Strange and Twisted Stories

Rebecca Henley aka AlairrialA

Table of Contents

Story 1

SHEILA...

CHAPTER 1

TWO WOMEN

Sheila was your average 22 year old young and vibrant woman. She lived with her friend Gayleigh. Often she would make dinner and do all the housework as she was unemployed whilst Gayleigh was employed full time by a beautiful woman who ran her own modelling business. Shiela was unfortunately born with a very severe mental health illness. This made it difficult for her to be able to live a normal life. She was suppose to take medications for her illness. But she decided after years of being on them that she no longer needed them. She found it very difficult to hold down a job. Sure! She had worked previously but due to the fact that she was unable to work with numbers without making many mistakes, she was soon forced to quit her job and join the unemployment lines. Sheila was made to feel unworthy by all those she met. All but her friend Gayleigh. Gayleigh found it very easy to be friends with Sheila as her mother also had a mental illness, manic depression. Gayleigh was a beautiful, young girl, at the ripe age of 16 she left home and moved in with her boyfriend

Alex. Not long after she had moved in with him, she felt there was something wrong between them. Sure enough! He was cheating on her. She moved out and into her own apartment soon after they split up due to his indiscretion. Gayleigh had a few more boyfriends and Sheila would often have sleep overs at her apartment. Gayleigh would retire with her boyfriend and Shiela would lie in bed and listen to the sounds coming from Gayleigh's room. She often wondered what it was that those boys did to make Gayleigh sound like that.

Shiela met Gayleigh when she was only 10 years old. She became good friends with her and they did everything together. As Sheila grew up, she and Gayleigh stayed as best friends and at the age of 17 she decided to leave home and move in with her. Shiela's mother, Doris, didn't think it was a good idea but Shiela had already made up her mind. Gayleigh had been in a terrible relationship, briefly, but long enough to make her best friend very unhappy. Sheila knew she could put a smile on Gayleigh's face mostly as a result of her stupid mistakes she seemed to be always making. Gayleigh just found the funny side and would snort when she laughed hard as Sheila told her the mistakes she'd made. This made Sheila feel very comfortable around Gayleigh.

Often Shiela's mother would give her a few words of wisdom. Sometimes she'd listen, act on what was said and other times she'd ignore her and look away as if she hadn't heard her. This is one of those times when Sheila decided to ignore the good advice she was being given from her mother. Sheila had already decided that she was going to be someone. She was going to be just like Gayleigh. A beautiful model, being paid a packet to stroll down a cat walk and wear stunning outfits and dresses and pants and swimsuits. Of course Sheila knew in her heart she wasn't pretty enough but hey! people can dream. Sheila would sit and listen to the strories her best friend told her and marvel at the perfection Gayleigh seemed to possess.

Gayleigh walked through the door, she was absolutely beaming and she walked over to Sheila and told her, "I'm going away". Sheila was heart broken, "How long for?" She asked Gayleigh. Gayleigh looked at the distress that must have come over Shiela's face. 'I've been offered a job in the states". Gayleigh was over pleased with this, Shiela thought, "but what about me?" Gayleigh took Sheila in her arms and gave her the biggest cuddle ever. "This is my dream", she said to Sheila. "If I don't grab this opportunity with both hands I could miss it entirely." "I want this!" Gayleigh wiped away the tears she had begun to cry. "You can come with me", she said. Sheila knew she couldn't. She wasn't pretty, she wasn't smart and she wasn't Gayleigh. She had her heart ripped from her chest as soon as Gayleigh uttered those words, she knew! She was being left behind. Sheila didn't cry. She couldn't find the tears to shed as she knew Gayleigh would be a fantastic model and she didn't want to stop her best friend from having her dream come true. Sheila said, " It's ok!' "I left home at 17, moved in with you and I'm 22 now." "You have been there for me all my life since I was 10". "It's time!" "Don't cry Gayleigh". "I'm so very proud of you, you'll be a star!". Gayleigh broke down in tears, she couldn't stop them from falling. The tears streamed down her face and dripped onto the blouse she was wearing. Sheila couldn't help but see the white blouse was getting wet which made it see through. Sheila was becoming aroused at the sight of her friend's perky breasts beginning to show through, she wasn't wearing a bra, she wondered why she hadn't felt this way before.

Sheila and Gayleigh went out to celebrate. They had a few too many drinks and on the way home in the taxi, Sheila kissed her. Gayleigh looked at her with eyes wide open and kissed her back. This was the beginning of a very special friendship. Sheila hadn't even thought about her best friend in this way before. She couldn't understand what made her feel this way now. She realised, "I'm in love with her". Sheila and Gayleigh got out of the taxi and walked, hand in hand up to the front door of the apartment building. The elevator was on ground floor and as the doors opened a woman stepped out, she excused herself and introduced herself as Cindy. She told Sheila that she lived in apartment 6. There was something perculiar about this woman, Sheila didn't know what but it was something. Sheila and Gayleigh walked to their door, opened it and stepped inside. "How rude". Sheila told Gayleigh. "It's as if she didn't even see you." Gayleigh nodded. "How, rude indeed".

Gayleigh told Sheila, "Go and have a lovely hot shower. "I'll pour a drink for us both and I'll join you shortly" Then we can put on something more comfortable if you like". Sheila was fully aroused by the time she entered the shower and before she could begin washing her body Gayleigh opened the shower screen door, looked at Sheila and stepped into the alcove. Sheila opened her arms and Gayleigh stepped into them. She was allowing the steaming hot water to flow down her beautiful, flawless body. Sheila knew she wanted to be with her. She never felt so sure of anything before in her life. Gayleigh was so beautiful and Sheila was just plain Jane. Sheila knew she wasn't pretty, but Gayleigh didn't care. Her lips were soft and supple. She found them very appealing and when they began kissing her neck, down her chest and over her, now very erect nipples, she couldn't help but swoon. She almost fell. Gayleigh caught her. She said "I'll never let you fall". "I will never let you down". "But I must leave in the morning". "Please come with me?" Sheila responded with a gentle caress on Gayleigh's buttocks, found her soft mound of scarcely unshaven hair and slipped her fingers inside her. Gayleigh let out a whisper of a moan and she felt her friend go weak at the knees. She dropped to hers and began kissing her friend's, now wet love spot. She didn't stop even when she felt her friend shudder then Gayleigh totally climaxed. It was beautiful. She had, for the first time in her life, made her friend very happy and there was no mistake. Gayleigh wasn't laughing or snorting. She was moaning and gasping and making those beautiful little sounds Sheila often heard when she was in her room with those boys. "Ah!", Sheila said to herself, "Thats what they were doing to make her sound like that".

Gayleigh and Sheila spent a very sensual and almost surreal evening together. Of course the alcohol they had consumed and continued consuming leading up to then had helped to enhance the actions they took. The sex was stimulating and the best sex, actually, the only sex that Sheila had partaken in. She, until that moment, had been a virgin. Gayleigh kissed and caressed Sheila's body and when they made love it was if they were one. Sheila fell into the love making so naturally, there wasn't any effort. It was as if they had been doing this all their lives. But it was the first and only time it would happen. Sheila knew this and decided to make it the best night to remember. It was! Shiela lay in Gayleigh's arms for the remainder of the night. She didn't want her best friend, now lover, to leave her but she knew she had to let her follow her dreams.

The next morning Gayleigh began packing and getting ready to leave. This would be the hardest thing both of them had to accept. The night they shared was something they would remember for the rest of their lives. Gayleigh wept whilst she packed. She knew she wouldn't see Sheila for a very long time. She was moving over 3000 miles away. They would keep in touch via internet, phone and video call but it wouldn't be the same. She knew there was no way they could be intimate at a distance. Sheila came into the room and sat at the foot end of her bed, staring at the exact spot they had previously made love. She turned her head away from Gayleigh and began to cry. Gayleigh took her by the shoulders and kissed her on the lips. She wiped away her tears and kissed her cheeks, her button nose and her forehead. It was magical, Sheila and Gayleigh wished this moment would last forever. Then Gayleigh moved aside and sat on the bed beside her.

Sheila turned away from her and said, "I love you!". Gayleigh replied, "ditto".

The yellow taxi pulled away from the apartment with Gayleigh waving through the window. Then it turned the corner and she was gone! Gayleigh had left to follow her dreams.

Sheila turned slowly and began to walk inside to pack. She couldn't stay where she was living as it was Gayleigh's apartment and now she was gone, she would have to somehow pay the rent. Without a steady job, this was going to be impossible. Even though Gayleigh told her to stay, she would pay the rent for her. She decided to leave.

Sheila packed what little possessions she had, it all fit into one suitcase, very sad for a 22 year old woman, she decided. Where was she going to go? What was she going to do? She had no idea, but she knew she wasn't going to move back home.

As she closed the door for the last time she looked up. Across the hall was the very lovely looking lady, from apartment 6, the same lady they met coming out of the elevator the night before. She was standing outside the elevator, waiting to go down, she knew Cindy. She eyed her for a brief moment and saw that she was quite tall, a pretty face and broad shoulders, quite manly actually. She remembered how rude she was to her friend. It was as if she was invisible. She decided she didn't quite like her. She was weird! But very beautiful regardless. She hadn't noticed this about her the night before when they met but then she didn't notice much of anything else either, she only had eyes for Gayleigh.

She asked Cindy to hold the elevator for her. She did. Sheila stepped inside and as the doors closed she felt the tears begin to fill her eyes and roll down her cheeks. She wiped them away, using her hand. "That's enough of that" She thought to herself.

Cindy and Sheila spoke briefly on the ride down. They discussed Gayleigh's fortunate turn of events and as they arrived at ground floor, they left the elevator with a hug and a plan to catch up later for a coffee. Sheila openly told Cindy about her sexual encounter with Gayleigh before she left and Cindy said it was lovely to hear of two women so much in love. "When am I going to get to meet this Gayleigh" Cindy asked. Sheila stared at her and replied. "You already have but you were so rude to her". Cindy. couldn't exactly remember when. Cindy seemed to Sheila to be hiding something. She didn't quite know what. But she knew it was something.

Whilst in the elevator Cindy told Sheila that she could possibly apply for a room just down the street at the old boarding house. It wouldn't be very expensive and she would have to share but at least she would have a roof over her head, company and good food to eat. She also knew of a position that opened up just down the road from the house, at a little cafe, they were looking for waitresses, maybe she could apply for a job there. Sheila agreed. She said she would head straight to the cafe and then the boarding house and if she wanted to catch up for coffee later, that's where she'd find her. Sheila applied for the waitressing job. Since she wouldn't be working with numbers she decided to give it a go. She got the job straight away. "Geez!" She said to herself, "They must be desperate".

CHAPTER 2

THE BOARDING HOUSE

The boarding house was nice looking from the outside and Sheila decided she could be quite happy living there. She didn't notice the bars on the windows. Sheila opened the front door. Inside she found a very well decorated room and a large wooden desk with a rather haughty looking woman sitting behind it doing her nails. She cleared her throat and with a small, squeaky voice, said "hello". The woman seemed to ignore her. She kept doing her nails and after what seemed quite a while Sheila spoke again. This time a little louder. "Hello". The woman looked up at Sheila and said, "There's no need to shout". Sheila felt a little flushed. She wasn't sure if it was anger or embarrassment that came over her but she was sure the woman could see that she had had an affect on her. She composed herself and said, "Hi!", "My name is Sheila, I'd like a room please". The woman eyed Sheila up and down and then said, "How long you staying?". Sheila replied, "Possibly forever."

Sheila lay down on her now, new bed. In her now, new room. She was tired. She had cried so much over the last few days and she was exhausted. She decided to have a quick shower and turn in for the night. She could worry about unpacking tomorrow and in the morning she was off to her new found employment. She was excited.

Sheila grabbed her soap, shower brush, gel, shampoo and conditioner and towel and headed for the communion bathroom. Being a boarding house she no longer had the use of her own bathroom but this was something she would have to get use to. As she was just about to head out the door her phone rang. It was her mum.

"Hi!" She heard her mum's voice. "How are you Sheila?". Doris hadn't even been told that Sheila wasn't living with Gayleigh anymore. Through the events that occurred leading up to Gayleigh leaving and the lovemaking she and Gayleigh had experienced. Sheila had totally forgotten to tell her mum that she wasn't going to be living in the apartment anymore. Or was it the fact that she knew only too well that Doris would demand she return home and that wasn't going to happen either. Not in Sheila's eyes anyway. She had just started to live a life on her own and this was the beginning of a brand new start.

Sheila replied, "Hi mum!". The conversation lasted for about an hour and after Sheila hung up she had filled her mum in on everything. Well nearly everything. She may have missed out the bit about her love making with Gayleigh. She knew Doris wouldn't understand. She was completely against anyone who was a homosexual or as Sheila said to Cindy, gay. Sheila told Doris that she was moving to a boarding house. That she'd secured a job in a cafe and her first shift was tomorrow. Doris wasn't exactly pleased to hear this and she asked, "When am I going to meet this Gayleigh?". "It seems you've been friends forever and hardly anyone has ever even seen her." Sheila could see what she was saying but she didn't have the answer she wanted to hear though. "I guess when she's visiting next I could arrange a trip to stay with you mum". "I'll run it past her next time we speak".

Sheila grabbed her toiletries, opened the door of her room and headed down the hallway to the bathroom. She undressed and found the laundry shute that the haughty woman, who's name was actually Tina, had told her about. The laundry was collected and delivered back to the roomies in the cost of their room. Sheila was actually quite pleased with this. However she did wonder how would each item of clothing be returned to each roomie if there wasn't any names etc on the clothes. She decided maybe there were individual shutes and each one came from the room they were in. "Hmmm." She even questioned that as she was standing in a shared bathroom. She felt a little confused but regardless, before even questioning this any further, she dropped her clothes in and heard them as they slid down the pipe to "Where?." She had no idea. She found the shower to be very refreshing and she stood under the water recounting the scenario that had taken place the night before, when she wasn't in the shower alone. She began to stroke her breasts, her hands caressed the tops of her thighs, she found herself becoming very aroused again, her nipples stood erect and she let her thoughts wander to Gayleigh. She wondered what she was doing and who was she with? Sheila finished herself off with the shower brush handle lathered in soap, that she had bought with her. She was surprised how diligent she was with her own body and wondered why she hadn't found herself this way, until now.

After what seemed a very long time, she stepped out of the shower and reached for her towel. A feeling of shock horror hit her. She'd forgotten it. She looked at her image in the steamed up mirror. "Oh shit". She declared. She was standing naked, her clothes were somewhere in the house and there was nothing to cover her naked body with. Not even a shower curtain. "Shit!". She repeated. She decided since it was very late at night and the house seemed very quiet, hoping they would all be asleep, that she would make a run for it. Sheila opened the door, looked out and seeing no one in the halls, she ran.

Once back in her room, panting wildly, Sheila grinned. "I made it." She said to herself with a giggle. All of a sudden she heard a noise. Sheila opened the door slowly and poked her head around the corner. Did anyone see her do her nudey run to her bedroom? She now wondered if she had been spotted running naked down the corridor. There was a small pool forming beneath her from the water that ran off her wet body. People's voices could be heard as she stood naked behind the door. She stepped back into her room, closed her door and reached for her towel. Dried herself off and put on her pj's. Sheila sat on her bed and looked around her room. She noticed a very antique looking mirror hanging on the wall.

When morning arrived she hadn't slept a wink. All night she lay awake with dread in her heart. "Was I seen?" She kept asking herself. She wasn't sure and this notion kept sleep from her. It evaded her like the plague. Every time she closed her eyes she could see the corridor down which she sprinted, naked as the day she was born. Her mother told her so many times on the phone the night before. "Don't forget your towel when you go to the shower".. She heard these words ringing in her ears.. Now it was time to face the day. The boarding house in which she lived was alive with the sounds of clattering, clunking, 'bang'; she heard the door next to her room slam.. 'Bang', the door slammed again. This made her jump almost out of her skin the first time and the second, well why was there a second? She thought. Then she heard angry voices coming from the room next door.. 'Who was it? A woman screamed! 'No one', she heard a whimpering man reply. 'It was no one'.. She hankered down between her sheets.. She'd been seen!

She listened as the voices got louder.. She glanced at the time on the clock on the wall. Her heart was pounding…

She was going to be late for work and it was her first day. She decided to put on a brave face. Got out of her safe haven of a bed and proceeded to choose her attire for the day. All the while the fighting which was ensuing in the next room didn't seem like abating any time soon. She hurriedly dressed in a comfortable pair of black slacks and a very pretty, yet rather promiscuous blouse. She knew she would be given an apron to wear once she arrived at her new job. She put on a comfortable pair of flats. "I'm going to be on my feet all day". She said to herself. Sheila diligently applied her make-up. 'Is this lipstick too dark?' she requested a reply from the inanimate mirror that hung from her wall… The mirror shook. 'Smash', it fell to the ground, shattering into a million pieces. Something or someone had hit the wall adjoining her room to where the couple were bantering like two school children over stolen lunch money. She grabbed her purse, her keys, scarf and hat and headed for the door. "I'll clean that up after work."

As she neared the doorway she glanced at the clock, which was still. 'Thank god', she sighed, affixed to the wall the mirror had dislodged from. It was given to her, by her, now deceased grandmother. The clock face revealed it was; she sighed again, extremely late.

Sheila tentatively opened her door and stood there for only a few seconds before taking flight and dashing past the door to the next room, she landed at the top of the stairwell and began the descent to the dining room where she was hoping to grab a quick cup of coffee before departing to her now, maybe ex-job, the boss hated anyone to be late and she had been told only yesterday by the woman who interviewed her, who's name was Rose, "Anyone, late for their duties, without reasonable explanation, will be FIRED!" "Oh my, she thought", "What will I do without a job now?"… She decided she would rather not think anymore of this concept… "I'll be fine", she uttered to herself, and "I'll have a good, reasonable explanation for my boss". She turned the corner that led into the dining room. Her hand flew to her face to cover her eyes. "OH MY GOD!" She let out a loud, spine tingling scream…

she couldn't believe the sight before her. There were all of her roomies sitting around the table and they were all "NAKED", she screamed this word out loud and before she knew it she was lying awake, on her bed. She sat bolt upright. Covered in sweat, that dripped down her face, over her button nose and onto her lips. She tasted the sweet, salty, droplets that seeped into her mouth. It took some time for her to realize that what she had just endured was in fact a dream. She asked herself, "Was the whole thing a dream? "Did I really dream all of this, the nudey run, the fighting next door, the smashed mirror, the whole lot? "Was this really a dream", she asked herself again and over and over. She glanced at the wall, the clock read 1/2 past 4. Sheila sat up and rubbed her eyes she was still wearing the same clothes she had on yesterday. "It was a dream!" She declared. After what seemed hours later when in actual fact was only a short time Sheila pulled up the sheet and blankets, rolled over and fell back to sleep fully clothed.

When Sheila woke, this time to begin her day, she rolled over and smiled, "It was just a dream!" She said to herself. She pushed back the sheets and blankets and sat up. Sheila ran her fingers through her hair, yawned and went to stand up. Then she saw it the mirror lay shattered in thousands of slivers of glass on the floor beneath the wall it had once hung upon. Sheila was confused, afraid and didn't know what to think. "It wasn't a dream!" She said to herself. She shivered all over. "It was real!".

CHAPTER 3

SHARD OF GLASS

Sheila stooped to begin picking up the glass from the smashed mirror. She didn't know what to think. She didn't know what had happened and all the while she wondered what lie waiting behind her bedroom door this morning?

She finished cleaning up the broken glass. When she had disposed of the shards of glass into the waste bin, wrapped in newspaper. She noticed a piece of paper that seemed to have been tucked inside the mirror frame. She reached for it and carelessly cut herself on a shard that had lodged itself in the carpet. She began to bleed quite profusely. "It must have been quite deep". She thought to herself. She reached for her towel. "Damn, it's white." The blood began to seep into the towel and the once white towel had now become red. As Sheila tried to stop the bleeding from her hand. She glanced again at the mirror frame and the piece of paper that was attached to it. She saw herself in the shard of glass. She screamed. What was staring back at her wasn't an image of herself, rather it was an old lady, wild looking, she had very weird, black eyes.

Sheila jumped up from where she was sitting, ran over to the window, looked out and did everything not to scream. It was then she noticed the bars on the window.

Sheila was staring at the bars when she heard a knock on the door. She froze. Whilst still holding the towel around her hand, she walked towards the door. "Who is it?" She asked. "Cindy." The woman replied. Sheila opened the door and let her in. She fell into her arms and cried.

CHAPTER 4

CINDY

Cindy was a kind and gentle woman. Sheila still felt that something was different about her and wondered what it could be. She felt like she had been run over by a steam roller. Her whole body ached and when she looked up into Cindy's face she didn't know what to say. She began to tremble. "What's wrong?". Cindy asked. "I don't know!". Sheila replied. Cindy noticed that Sheila was still gripping to the once white, now red, towel in her hand. "What happened?" She asked Sheila. Sheila told Cindy that the mirror had fallen off the wall, smashed into millions of shards of glass and as she reached for a piece of paper that was stuck inside the frame, she accidentally swiped her hand across a shard of glass jutting out of the carpet. Cindy looked at her with bewilderment. "Which mirror?". Cindy asked. Sheila pointed towards the place on the wall where the mirror once was. To her amazement it was there. The mirror that had fallen off the wall was there. Intact and still hanging in the exact same place it was when she entered the room. Sheila fainted.

When Sheila came around Cindy was sitting next to her on the bed. She had picked Sheila up and put her into bed. Sheila looked at the mirror. It was still hanging on the wall. She recounted the whole entire story to Cindy beginning with the shower and ending with the mirror. Cindy looked confused. "But the mirror is still there!". "I know!." Said Sheila. "I don't know!". She too was confused.

Sheila decided to ring her mum. She wanted to hear a friendly voice and she just wanted it to be hers. Cindy passed her the phone and she dialled the number. Doris answered. "Hello". Sheila began crying. "Mum", "I don't know what is going on!". Doris heard the desperation in her daughter's voice. "Are you ok?, "I haven't heard from you for a while now". "I was beginning to get worried about you". "Are you ok?" Sheila looked at Cindy. Sheila replied, "Mum, I spoke to you last night", "I was heading for the shower when you rang and we spoke for at least an hour". "Don't you remember?".

Doris went quiet. "I haven't spoken to you for a couple of days now, Sheila." "Where's Gayleigh?" "May I speak with her?". and then Sheila heard what she didn't want to hear. "Are you taking your meds?". Sheila told her mum she was fine, she was taking her meds, and she'd call her back later. Then hung up. Cindy looked at Sheila with a look of bewilderment. "I thought you said you spoke to Doris last night". "I thought I did" said Sheila.

Sheila thanked Cindy and asked her to accompany her to the cafe. Cindy told Sheila she would buy them both a coffee. Sheila wondered if she had dreamt everything. The shower, the mirror, then she saw the towel. It was red from the blood and yet there was no wound on her hand.

"What the fuck is happening?" She asked the mirror on the wall. The image of her face turned into the old woman she saw before in the shard of glass. She screamed and hit the floor. Cindy who had just stepped out to use the bathroom, came running into the room. "What's wrong?". "What happened?". Sheila sat on the floor with her hands over her eyes and just cried.

CHAPTER 5

THE MIRROR

When Sheila had calmed down and once again told Cindy the whole story, she got to her feet, looked in the mirror and saw her face staring back at her. Cindy stood next to her. She prompted Sheila to take her meds and get ready for work. Sheila did as she was told. Sheila put on the exact same clothes that she had done in her dream. She told Cindy, who now looked even more manly than before, that she possibly could have missed one of her doses and that's the reason for all this delusional behaviour. Deep down she knew she hadn't. She never has and never will. But the explanation seemed to have the desired affect. They left to walk to the cafe.

As Sheila passed the mirror on the wall she took one last glance, there she was, the old woman staring back at her, her eyes were even blacker than before. Sheila closed the door and locked it. She took Cindy by the hand, which didn't feel like a woman's hand, and walked to and out the front door.

As they passed the house, Cindy asked, "What's with the bars?" Sheila shrugged and kept walking.

CHAPTER 6

THE CAFE

Sheila arrived just in time for her first shift. She was shown the ropes by Rose and told if she does a good job she'll be rostered on for more shifts, this pleased Sheila.

Cindy ordered a cup of coffee and sat at a table outside the cafe, she lit up a cigarette and began to puff away at it. She wasn't lady like at all. Sheila delivered her coffee to her and couldn't help but notice the facial features on her new found friend's face.

She gasped. "She's not a woman!". She said to herself. "She's a man!"

Cindy grabbed Sheila's hand and beckoned her to take a seat. Sheila glanced over at her boss and as she wasn't at the front counter decided to sit for a few minutes. If she was seen she'd probably receive a rousting. Sheila didn't care. Cindy was a man!

Cindy explained to Sheila that she/he was indeed a man. He was a cross dresser. He confided in her that he wanted to be a woman so badly that he took on the persona of one.

Cindy was the name of his pet dog when he was a child and as he grew up he decided that he enjoyed being a girl more than being a boy. Sheila felt for him. She told him his secret was safe with her.

Sheila's boss came over to where Sheila and Cindy were sitting. She said to Sheila, " I'm not paying for you to sit around and fratinise with the customers". "Get up and serve those people over there!". Shiela stood up and glanced over to where Rose was pointing. There she was. Sitting at the table. The old woman she saw in the mirror. Then when she looked away and looked again, she was gone. Sheila shook her head and headed over to the young woman and young man waiting to be served.

At the end of the day Sheila's feet were hurting. They were feeling sore and she couldn't wait to be off them. She couldn't wait to get home and make a cup of tea, put her feet up and maybe have a nap. She handed in her apron and said goodbye to Rose. Sheila walked out the door and into the street. When she looked over at the adjacent corner, there she was. The old woman was staring back at her. She trembled and began to walk faster. She had almost broken into a run when a car sped across in front of her. She stopped. Across from her, on the opposite corner, was the old woman. This time she didn't look away. She just stared her down and Sheila became frightened. This woman looked evil and yet familiar.

Sheila arrived at the gate of the boarding house. The front doorstep had been freshly painted so she had to gain entry by walking around the back. As she went through the side gate she glanced into the window on the side of the house. "Where are the bars?" She thought to herself. There weren't any on that window. Actually there weren't any on any other window, but hers! "Weird!" She said to herself.

CHAPTER 7

DINING WITH ROOMIES

After Sheila had settled into her room for the mean time, before dinner, she had a chance to recount what had been spoken about with Cindy earlier on. "Wow!" "She's really a man". She said out loud. The phone rang. It was Gayleigh. Sheila felt so relieved. She answered with a cheery "Hi". Gayleigh, straight away, knew something was wrong. How, Sheila didn't know, she asked. "What's happened?" Sheila couldn't fool her best friend. She told her the whole incredulous story from beginning to end. Gayleigh was taken back by what Sheila was saying. Gayleigh didn't know what to say to her friend. She didn't know how to explain what was happening. Then Sheila recounted her conversation with Cindy. Gayleigh was shocked. She too had been under the impression that Cindy was a woman. This seemed to disturb her friend greatly. Sheila asked, " Gayleigh are you jealous?" Gayleigh laughed, that familiar snort was heard on the other end of the phone. "Just a little." She giggled. "No need to be." Sheila said. "I love you, and only you!" Gayleigh replied, "Ditto".

26

After Sheila got off the phone to Gayleigh, she glanced at the clock on the wall. It read 6.00, it was time for dinner. This would be the first meal Sheila had actually shared with her roomies. She didn't even think anymore about 'her dream'. She headed down the stairs into the dining room.

She remembered the vision she saw in her dream, all the roomies sitting around the breakfast table naked. She grimaced at the thought. When she turned the corner and entered the dining room, she was met by a rather handsome looking young man and a lovely looking young girl standing next to him. They were standing in the doorway to the dining room. Sheila excused herself and introduced herself to the young couple.

"Oh! We know who you are." The young man said. "You're the streaker". Sheila felt her breath leave her body. She HAD been seen. The rest of the roomies were seated at the dining table and as she entered the room she was glared at and stared at by everyone. There was, by counting, 12 people seated for dinner. Tina amongst them and a man who Sheila assumed to be her husband. "Well!", "Well!" "Well!" Tina scowled at Sheila.

"Rules of the house, no streaking!" and then began to laugh very loudly in which everyone joined in. Even Sheila had a giggle even though it was at her own expense.

The evening went off without a hitch. Sheila was now known as 'the streaker'.

After dinner Sheila had full intentions of asking her host if there was a story attached to the mirror which hung on the wall in her room. The old man sitting opposite her caught her attention. "Did you hear the sound of breaking glass last night?" He directed his question towards her. Sheila froze. "What?" She replied. The old man who Sheila had come to know as Harold repeated the question. "Did you hear the sound of breaking glass last night?" He repeated it slowly. It was later revealed that Harold and his wife Clara occupied the room next to hers. Sheila excused herself from the dining table and headed to her room. She couldn't begin to explain what had happened. "Was it a dream?". She asked herself? "Was it real?" She asked again. "What the?" She couldn't find any answers.

As Sheila put the key in the lock she thought she heard a rustling from inside her room. She froze. She listened with her ear pressed hard up against her door. There it was again. Someone was in her room.

Sheila left her doorway and headed for the stairs. There she met another roomie. His name was Darius. She asked Darius to come to her room with her. Darius must have gotten the wrong idea and smiled. He had rotten teeth. Actually he was quite unsightly, ugly for a better word. "No!", "I don't mean that way." Sheila felt repulsed at the thought of his dirty hands touching her, but she needed someone to check out her room and he was it. Darius looked disgusted when Sheila explained that she heard a noise coming from inside her room. It was then that he realised he wasn't going to get his end in. He followed her to her room and she unlocked her door, pushed it open slowly. As they stepped into the room they both heard a sound of running feet on the floor. But! The room was empty. No one was there. Darius sneered at Sheila and headed back out the door. "Prick teaser", he scowled. "Bloody Sheila". Sheila couldn't help but smirk at his disgust and replied "Yes!" "That's me!" "Sheila that is and I'm no prick teaser", "I don't even like men". This intrigued Darius even more and told Sheila "Mmmmm", "I like a bit of girl action". "I'm off now to lighten my load". He laughed as he walked out the door. Sheila ran and closed the door rather harshly, it slammed shut. The sound reverberated through the entire house. "Oops!", "My bad?" Sheila giggled to herself.

CHAPTER 8

NOISES IN THE NIGHT

Sheila had a quick shower, this time remembering to take her towel with her and what seemed to be becoming a routine slap and tickle session each time she showered, Sheila again finished herself off with the lathered up handle of the shower brush. "Hmmmm!" She said to herself, "I must invest in a vibrator". This shower brush isn't quite hitting the spot anymore." She was rather amused as she hadn't even considered anything like that before.

Sheila headed back to her room, as she approached her doorway she heard the familiar sound that she'd heard earlier on. This time as it was quite late and everyone seemed to be in their rooms, Sheila decided to put her big girl panties on and investigate the noise herself. As she put the key in her door she could hear soft voices, whispers, from inside her room. She threw open the door and the voices stopped.

Sheila turned on the light and looked around. There was nothing to be seen. However she did notice a rope tied to her bed head, "That wasn't there before", she gasped as she tried to understand the implications as to what it meant and where it came from.

Sheila untied the rope. Threw it in the waste bin, there it was! The newspaper with the shards of glass still wrapped inside. She drew the parcel out of the bin and began unwrapping it. The shards of the broken mirror weren't there. It was the red towel filled with blood. She quickly rewrapped the parcel and threw it back into the bin. "Am I going insane?" She asked herself. "What the?" Sheila climbed into her bed, turned of the bedside lamp, rolled over and fell asleep.

Sheila woke with a start. She had been awoken by a blood curdling scream. She thought it had come from somewhere in the house but she couldn't be sure. She climbed under her bed covers and tried to fall back to sleep. "It's none of my bees wax". She used to be told this by her daddy when she was just a little girl. Before he died at his own hand and left mummy a widow. Whenever she tried to say anything to him that resembled gossip or someone else's business was the topic of the conversation, her father used to say, "It's none of your bees wax". This was one of those times she thought, "You're right daddy". "You're so right!".

Sheila heard strange noises all night every night whilst living in the boarding house but no sound was more eerier than the sound that woke her this one particular night.

She was lying in bed and was just about to turn out the light when the sound of her door opening startled her. She was absolutely certain she locked it. She froze under the covers and waited for them to be ripped off or a hand to touch her, or worse.

She didn't know what to do or how to react. She waited with baited breath. When she realised she'd actually stopped breathing she started to breathe again. But not before she could hear another type of breathing in her ears. She wasn't alone.

Sheila waited for the presence in her room to attack her. It never came. It would breathe heavily in her ears and then nothing! The whole scenario would stop and begin again the next night and the next. This continued for at least a month.

Every day Sheila would get up after a rough night's sleep or lack of and head off to work. She would quite often meet with Cindy and have a coffee at the cafe. Her boss became quite friendly. Yes! She was sleeping with the boss. Never in her wildest dreams did she think that her life would be being lived this way. Sex on tap! Great job. Good friends. Her roomies had at last warmed up to her and she was quite the popular one in the house.

Sheila was living. Gayleigh would phone regularly and Sheila would recount the events that occurred within that week to her. They would stay on the phone for hours. Gayleigh always replied with "Ditto", whenever Sheila told her she loved her. Then all of a sudden she didn't ring anymore. Gayleigh had been killed in a car crash on her way to a fashion show. Sheila was devastated. She wanted to take her own life and knew Gayleigh wouldn't want that for her. So instead she turned to drugs to ease the pain of her heart being broken.

CHAPTER 9

THE FUNERAL

"Gayleigh was my friend". "My lover". The entire congregation gasped. No one knew! Sheila was telling them something they had no idea about and that wasn't ok. Sheila continued. "Gayleigh took me under her wing at the age of 10 years old." "No one wanted to know me because of my mental illness." "But Gayleigh didn't care." "She accepted me for me and I loved her". Sheila tried to wipe away the tears she couldn't stop from falling. Her whole world had collapsed with the loss of her dearest friend, one time lover. After the epitaphs had been delivered it was time for the viewing.

Sheila wanted to be the first to say goodbye. Until now it had been surreal. Sheila didn't know what to say, what to do, it just didn't seem real. She wished it wasn't. She wanted her friend back.

Sheila walked up the aisle to where the casket lie open. She closed her eyes and approached it. She opened her eyes and screamed. The body lying in the casket wasn't her friend she had grown to love, it was the body of the old woman she had seen in the mirror. She screamed again. She ran out of the church and kept running. Sheila felt like her heart had been ripped out of her chest. Not only had she lost her best friend but now she didn't even get to say goodbye to her. "And who is that woman in her casket?" Sheila ran all the way home. When she arrived at the boarding house it was in complete darkness. She ran up the front steps, through the door, up the stairs to her room. She threw the key into the lock, unaware of the voices behind the door. She threw herself on her bed and cried. She cried and cried, she cried so much that her throat began to hurt. She got off her bed and stood up. She walked over to the mirror hanging on the wall, looked into it and begged it to tell her what she wanted to hear. That it is all just a dream! The mirror remained silent. She then became aware of the voices that were gathering in the room. They became louder and louder until her whole room was filled with whispers and then she saw it. The image in the mirror had changed, it wasn't her face looking back at her. It was Gayleigh's. Not the beautiful face she remembered but an ugly old woman's face that resembled that of the old woman who haunted her. Gayleigh's face was evil, it had blackened eyes and the features of a witch. Sheila passed out. She hit the floor with a thud. There was banging on the door but she didn't hear it. No one was able to save her. The presences in the room all swarmed over and around Sheila's limp body. Sheila had the breath sucked out of her lungs. Sheila was dead.

CHAPTER 10

GAYLEIGH

Cindy raced to the boarding house, somehow he knew. Darius was banging on the door when Cindy arrived. The host had bought the spare key to the room and Cindy put the key in the door. It turned and the lock clicked. The three outside the door could hear many voices behind the door and wondered who was in the room with her. The door was thrown open and the voices stopped. Cindy was the first to step into the room and Darius the second, followed by Tina. Lying on the floor in front of the smashed mirror was Sheila's body. She was white as a ghost. The glass has severed her throat and she was lying in a pool of blood. Cindy rushed to her side. Darius, squeamish from the sight of the blood, slunk back into the corner and covered his eyes with his filthy, dirty hands. Tina stood next to Cindy and put her hand on his shoulder. It was then she noticed the small piece of paper stuck inside the frame. She leant down and drew it out. She uncrumpled it and was shocked to see it was a portion of a photograph. She gave it to Cindy. There staring back at him was the image of

Sheila. Not the young Sheila they all grew to love but an old evil looking woman with blackened eyes and wild hair.

"How's this at all possible?" Asked Tina. "It's not" replied Cindy. "And yet here she is". Said Tina. "I know", replied Cindy.

Sheila's body was sent to be cremated a week after she had died. Her mother came to the funeral along with Cindy, Tina, Darius and Rose. After the service Cindy, who had now reverted back to his former self Clark, approached Doris. He offered his condolences and asked her if they could have a chat. Doris agreed.

Clark began by saying how beautiful her daughter was and that she was a very special woman. Even though he hadn't actually met her best friend, one time lover Gayleigh, he believed her to be beautiful also just by the way Sheila spoke about her.

Doris flinched. "You've never met Gayleigh either?" She sounded surprised. Clark was taken back by this response. "How is this possible?" Asked Clark. "You know they met when she was 10 years old and then she moved in with her at 17 until she turned 22". "That's when she became her lover, just before she left to pursue her modelling career." "Then she died as a result of a car accident." "She even went to her funeral".

"How could you have never met this woman?" "You're her mother".

Doris began by explaining that as a child Sheila had been born with severe mental difficulties. Her brain never actually developed as other children her age did.

At the age of 10 she developed a psychosis and she began speaking to imaginary people. "I think one of these may have been Gayleigh". Clark was shocked. Doris continued on. She told Clark that at the age of 17 she disappeared after not having the correct medication which was meant to counteract the delusions she was having. Doris went on to tell Clark that her daughter lived alone in her apartment and that she didn't have any friends, only the ones which lived inside her mind. Clark felt a stab of pain as if a knife had pierced his chest. He realised, all along, that Sheila and Gayleigh were the same person. It struck him as he remembered what she said about their love making session. "It's as if they were one". Doris began to explain to Clark further about her daughter's illness. The delusions she would have and the voices she would hear. She told him of seperate occasions when she would be found sitting in the corner after saying that 'they' attacked her. There was no 'they' Doris revealed. At times she would be found with a knife ready to slash her own throat. It's then that the image of Sheila lying on the floor in a pool of blood came back to haunt Clark.

"That's how she died you know!" Clark told Doris. "Her throat was slashed with the shards of glass from a broken mirror." "Did you know that we found a photograph tucked into the frame after it was smashed?" Clark asked Doris. "No!" Doris replied. "Have you got it now?" "Yes!". Said Clark. He pulled the portion of the photograph out of his pocket and gave it to Doris. When Doris looked at it, what she saw staring back at her was impossible. It was a face that resembled her daughter's. The face wasn't young and pretty it was old, hard looking, with wild hair. She was looking at a woman who had been through hell and back. The photo was definitely that of her daughter, Sheila. "How's this possible?" She asked Clark. Clark replied. "Maybe we aren't all who we seem to be." "Maybe Sheila's delusions were real". "Maybe she was being attacked and the whole time she was seen as psychotic." "Maybe". Doris said. Clark asked Doris, "Do you take any medications for any illnesses yourself?". Clark found himself very curious. "Yes!" "I have a mental illness, manic depression. It was developed whilst I was carrying Shiela."

He took the photograph back from Doris, took a lighter out of his pocket and lit it on fire. Doris bid Clark goodbye and headed off to join the congregation. They were dissipating into cars and on foot. The cemetery became a quiet and lonely place to be.

Clark decided the secrets that Sheila kept were to die with her. The woman he met wasn't crazy. She wasn't psychotic and she didn't need any more people to think she was.

As Clark was walking through the cemetery he happened to notice the name on one of the tomb stones as he was passing by. 'Here lies Gayleigh Thorpe'. 'Beloved wife of Darius Thorpe', 'Loving mother of two beautiful daughters Rose and Tina.'

'Killed suddenly in a fatal car crash.' 'Taken much too soon.' 'Gayleigh will be sadly missed by all who loved her.' 'RIP beautiful soul.' 'May you sleep with the angels in heaven.'

'Born 1902- Died 1999.' Her picture was on the tombstone. What stared back at Clark was the photo of the woman he had just set on fire. Clark was right to say that maybe she wasn't crazy after all. Maybe she was already dead. Clark kept walking. He would always remember the woman he met as Sheila.

The boarding house still takes in travellers and homeless people. Tina kept Sheila's secret, along with Darius, Rose and of course Clark.

Many months went by and along came another free spirited woman. She sat on her bed listening to the sounds inside the boarding house. On the wall of her room, hung an old antique mirror. It was pretty to look at and looked very old.

The young girl got up from her bed and walked over to the mirror. She looked into it.

All that was heard from the rooms inside the house, was the shattering of glass and a blood curdling scream that came from the room of the free spirited traveller. Darius was the first one to her door.

The end.

COMPLETED May 17/19

CHILDREN'S WHISPERS

CHAPTER 1

THE HOUSE

My parents bought our house way back when it was affordable to buy houses. Now! It's almost impossible to afford to buy a house. Especially one like this!

Our house stood out amongst all the other houses on the street. It was grand looking with shutters on the windows and a bold, blue, front door. This one had gained a name for itself. No one wanted to buy it. This one was known to be occupied by a group of 4 ghost children. 'Mischevious little imps' they were known as to the community. What we didn't know was that there would be more to this story than what met our own eyes. This story is one that will remain in our memories for a lifetime. If we all survived that long to tell it.

It was mid March, 17 years ago, when they received the phone call saying "It's yours!", "Congratulations", they heard the bank manager say over the phone. "You can move in as early as the end of this month if you like!" "Yes please!" Tracey replied. "Thank you for everything!" The bank manager let out a loud laugh. "Oh! It's totally my pleasure!" "Enjoy your new home, all of you!" By all of us I thought he meant my Mother Tracey who was a wonderful person, she gave to everyone. No one missed out, that is everyone but me. My father Frank, he drank every night and would beat my mother behind closed doors. Then there was my little sister, Trissy, that's what I called her, her real name was Patricia, she was only 2. Oh! and I couldn't forget my brother, ohhhhh my brother! His name was Max, he was 16. Twice my age and twice as nasty to go with it. He wasn't a brother anyone would want to have wished upon them. He was my worst nightmare. He would lock me inside a cupboard and only let me out when I would agree to his stupid terms and he would only allow me to sit with him and watch TV when I would agree to stupid things he asked me to do. Like getting him popcorn and drinks and letting him put his hand up my skirt. He didn't love me. He hated me for being alive. Trissy was my favourite and everyone knew it. Everyone that is, except Trissy.

CHAPTER 2

MOVING DAY

This house was our parent's dream. They had been saving every cent all their adult lives. I would have been turning 8 when we moved in and my mother said I could have the room with the view. By this she meant the room with the window that overlooked the grave yard. You see! This house was built on the edge of one and from the window in my room I could see all the graves and tomb stones, including the 4 little white crosses that stood at the edge. They didn't quite look right! "It looks like no one loved them". I thought to myself as I looked out my new bedroom window.

How right I was! Little did anyone know what sort of mishaps and accidents we were destined from the moment we closed that big, blue front door and the house became ours. They didn't like us! They, as in the 4 children who lived inside my lounge room fireplace. The children no one else could see, no one that is but me. Oh and Trissy.

It all began one very cold winter morning. My father decided to put some wood in the lounge room fireplace. He stepped outside to go and chop some. The wind that blew in as soon as he opened our front door was freezing. "Brrrrrr", I heard my mother say. "Shut that bloody door". I ran over and closed the door behind my father. I thought I heard it lock but I couldn't be sure. When my father had finished chopping the wood he stood in front of the door, arms loaded up and kicked it. He couldn't knock with his arms full. I raced to the door, turned the handle and tried pulling it open. It wouldn't. It WAS locked. I could hear my father ranting and raving from behind the door. "Open this bloody door now!" he yelled. "I'm trying". I screamed back. I could just imagine how cold my father was getting and I tried everything to open the door but it wouldn't budge. That's the first time I felt weird about the house. I remembered thinking, "I thought I heard it lock" and now I was sure. It did! After what seemed quite some time I managed to open the door. It just 'unlocked', on its own. I know this sounds really stupid and when I say it, it sounds even sillier but I swear I could hear the slightest of giggles in the air around me.

CHAPTER 3

FATHER

I pulled open the door and there on the doorstep was my father. I decided not to tell him that it was locked and no one locked it but It was. I said, "it was jammed, I think!" My father was angry and I knew what that meant. He ranted and raved and talked to himself as he was piling the wood into the fireplace. "I'll take a look at it tomorrow". "Bloody house!" I sat back and watched as he went on a rampage looking for matches to light the fire with. I thought, "how strange", "I could have sworn there was a box on the mantle". Father always kept one there in the other house. He didn't like it when he couldn't find things he knew had a place to be in.

When he came storming back into the lounge room with a box of matches in his hand. He tripped over, what? There was nothing there to trip over. He hit his head, quite hard, on the ground. "almost knocked meself out", "bloody big feet". I looked at him. I was absolutely bewildered as to what just happened. He got to his feet and headed over to the fireplace.

"I'm thinking" he said, "I'm going to get a locksmith in tomorrow and check out that bloody front door". I knew, somehow, he wouldn't find anything wrong with it. I didn't say what I knew.

Father was a man who would often talk to himself and argue with my mother every time something went wrong. I think it gave him power or something. I didn't like the way he would come home, stumble inside after a full night of drinking and if things weren't exactly right, to his liking, like the dishes weren't done, his dinner wasn't on the table and other littler things like a fire wasn't lit, if it was cold, so he could sit and be lazy in front of it whilst having his dinner and watching tv. My father was a bully!

This one particular night he came home, after he had the front door looked at by a very expensive locksmith, the only one in town, so he wasn't able to shop around. He put the key in the lock and tried to turn it. It wouldn't turn. He stood out on the front step. We could hear him fumbling with the key and I ran to the door, opened it and let him in. I thought to myself, "should just leave you outside", "at least no one would get hurt tonight". I guess I knew what was in store. He'd been heavily drinking and today, as a result of my mother's depression she had sunk into from being badly treated by my father, hadn't done the dinner, or the dishes. "Father is going to be pissed!" "In more ways than one" I said to myself.

I ran to my room. I didn't want to be there when he started and I wanted to keep Trissy safe. Trissy was sitting on her bed. I walked into her room and closed the door behind me, I reached for her earphones that were lying on her bedside table and put them, gently, into her ears. I knew the shouting would begin very soon. I didn't know what else to do. I was only 8. I heard the banging of doors, first I heard the bedroom door, then the chest of drawers opening and closing, the sound of a suitcase being zipped up amongst shouting and then the front door slammed. He was gone! I never saw my father again after that night. He left us! All of us! I wasn't angry or upset. A little relieved, to be honest. Enough was enough! "I'll look after my family," I said to myself. "I can and I will!" I closed my eyes, rolled over and fell asleep.

CHAPTER 4

MOTHER

My mother would often just lie in her bed until it was time to get up, as I had mentioned earlier, she was suffering from depression. My father was the cause of this and to a point I would have been too.

She wasn't herself today. She wasn't herself any day but today especially. My mother liked everyone and as I also said before, everyone but me. My mother was a strange woman. She would get up every morning and put the kettle on. Make breakfast but never use the kettle. Just boil it. I got used to her doing this and it wasn't something that bothered me anymore. That was until I walked into the kitchen this morning and found her with the kettle, she was filling it and the water was overflowing. I ran over to the sink and switched off the tap. I took the kettle from my mother's hands and tipped some out, put the kettle back in its place and switched it on at the wall. I felt a buzz from the switch. Not anything to hurt me, just a buzz. My mother sat at the table and as a result of last night's fight, I could see where my father had struck her, countless times. She had a bruised cheek and a black eye. I felt sorry for my mother but she didn't like me to. She would often tell me that this was her choice. I thought to myself, "Who in their right mind, would choose a life like this?" But I never asked.

This particular morning I had already gotten Trissy up and toileted here. She was now snoring her head off back in her bed. I decided not to disturb her and left her asleep.

My brother was gloating, over his phone, to his mate how he had cheated on his test and how the teacher had given him an A as a result of not knowing he cheated. I hated my brother. He was always the smart one. "But I'd never cheat" I said to myself. Everyone was there. Everyone but my father. He hadn't returned after last night. I thought, "good riddance," and continued on preparing my breakfast whilst listening to my brother rant about his score he received from being dishonest.

CHAPTER 5

MAX

My brother Max, as I mentioned before was 16. He had a very big fan club with all his mates and they all thought he was a wonderful guy. But he wasn't. I thought if they knew what he did when the lights went out they would change their minds as quick as overnight. But they would never find out. Or so I believed.

This particular morning he was sitting, as I said, on his phone. I could hear him telling his mates, on conference call, that he had cheated the system and got an A from the teacher. He was smug and for that I truly hated him. He was going on and on about how he did it. All of a sudden the phone burst into flames and burnt his ear. "Holy shit". I heard him yell. "What the hell happened?". I knew! I could hear the distinct giggles in the air. I just knew!.

CHAPTER 6

TRIXIE, MISSY, ADAM, TROY & BEN

I arrived at school and was sitting on the bench waiting to go into class. I was listening to a story that a kid was telling to a group of kids. He wasn't aware that I was sitting there or at least I didn't think he was.

"They died". I heard him say. "All of them!" He continued. No one knew how or when, they were just found, one by one in the cellar, over a period of 4 weeks". "One by one they disappeared and one by one they were found there!" It was then I heard what sent a shiver down my spine. "Where?" I heard a boy ask the kid telling the story. "In the house with the big blue door".

I was stuck to my seat, I couldn't move. The most horrible thought stuck in my head. "The house with the big blue door". "That's our house!" I screamed inside.

The boy looked in my direction and I knew he knew who I was. He grinned, a horrible looking grin, he showed his teeth and it made him look like a dog who was ready to rip something or someone apart. It bought back a terrible memory. I pushed it aside and just at that moment the bell rang. It was time to go to class.

"What was he saying to them?" I thought to myself. "Is that the 4 little white crosses I saw in the graveyard?" I decided to ask one of the kids, I found out later, called Trixie. I met up with her in the halls. She was a cute kid, pig tails that fell down her back and blonde hair, that if I didn't know any better, I'd say looked fake, dyed even. I found out that she was 8 just like me. I spoke with her briefly, in passing, I asked her "what was that kid telling you this morning in the yard?" She said, "something about a group of kids who were killed, found in the cellar of a house with a big blue door." "Don't know really!" She hurried off, quite rudely, I thought. She yelled back over her shoulder. "You live there don't you?" She laughed and kept walking.

A little while later I was walking down the hall when a boy headed me off. He was tall and I'd say about 10 years old. I sort of remembered him from another class and I think it was a couple of grades up from me. He stood in front of me and started to stroke my face. He told me "hi!" "I'm Ben". "You must be Max's little sister". "He's right, you are cute". A feeling of dread came over me. He knew my brother and I'm guessing he told him what he did to me after dark. I tried to move aside and he kept stepping with me. He said, "I've been watching you!" I felt a little scared by this time and I asked him to please move out of my way. He looked at me, leaned in to kiss me and said "if you can give it to him, you can give it to me!" I turned around and ran. I didn't want anyone to know what my brother was making me do, every night, and here he is telling everyone.

I was crying. I found a corner to slink into and I slid down the wall. Whilst sitting on the floor I put my hands over my face and let out the biggest scream.

A boy, I think he was my age, maybe he could've even been in my class, leaned down and pulled my hands away from my face. He sat next to me. I then recognised him from the group the kid was telling stories to. He began comforting me with an arm around my shoulder and said, "Hi", "I'm Adam" "and you must be?" Until now I haven't even told you my name and now I realised that I could be anyone I wanted to be. I always wanted to be known as special so I told him and I'm telling you, my name is "Gem". I looked at him. He looked me in the eyes and said "that's a pretty name" is it short for something?" I told him. "Gemima". "But I don't like that name so please call me Gem". "Ok!" "Gem it is!" "Thank you Adam". "I like that name, by the way." "Thanks" said Adam. We sat in the corner until a teacher found us and told us to "go back to class" in a rather loud, unforgiving voice. We did as we were told. I liked Adam, but he seemed a little too nice. Regardless I knew we would meet again.

Lunch time came and a younger girl, than me, came up to the table I was sitting at and sat down in front of me. I looked up from eating my lunch and found her staring at me, she seemed to be staring into my soul. I could feel her eyes boring into me and I felt uneasy. She said, in a quite soft voice, "Stay away from him". Her voice was so quiet I almost missed what she had said. I replied, "I'm sorry!" "I didn't quite hear you." "You we're saying?" "STAY AWAY FROM TROY." she screamed and ran away before I could even make sense of what was happening. Later that day I was told, by another kid, that her name was Missy. "Wow!" "I'm really not very popular in this school, am I?" But I didn't really care. I had much worse things to worry about. Like my brother.

CHAPTER 7

THE KETTLE

Tracey did her usual thing. She climbed out of bed and headed into the kitchen. She filled the kettle up and put it on to boil. She began to get the toast ready and got the butter and condiments out of the fridge. Then all of a sudden she turned around when she heard the kettle pop. She walked over to it and stared at it. Something told her to lift it up and pour the water on her hand. Tracey screamed as the boiling hot water gushed over her hand and saw it becoming read, blistered and swelling. She couldn't stop. She tried to but something or someone had hold of the kettle and wouldn't let her put it down. She passed out onto the floor. The kettle dropped onto the counter.

When I ran into the kitchen after hearing my mother's scream I was shocked to find her lying on the floor. Her hand had been scolded, beyond recognition, her fingers were peeled and the lack of skin on her hand revealed her bones. "What happened?" I screamed at her. By this time she had begun to gain consciousness. She was trying to tell me, through her tears, something about the kettle. I couldn't quite understand what she was saying. Something about the kettle being possessed. I looked at it sitting back on the plate and wondered why had my mother placed it there especially when it was after she had burnt her hand. Then those little whispers and giggles, the ones I was getting used to hearing now, began again. I knew! I just knew!

CHAPTER 8

4 LITTLE WHITE CROSSES.

Once my mother's hand had been seen to and dressed by the nurses at the GP clinic. The hospital wasn't as close as the clinic to our house. I was told it would have to have specialised burn treatment. When asked what happened. I didn't exactly know what to say. I remembered my mother saying something about the kettle being possessed. I couldn't tell the doctor that, they'd think we were both crazy and so I told them, "I'm really not too sure." "I heard her scream and found her on the floor" I left out the part about the kettle being back on the plate. That just sounded too weird and would provoke more questions as to why she placed it back there after she'd burnt herself.

But I knew! I just knew!

Once I had arrived back home with my mother, I sent her to lie down and I headed upstairs to my bedroom. I passed Max's doorway and saw him lying on his bed with his earphones in and listening to music. I wanted to scream at him about the thing that happened at school but I didn't have the energy. Trissy was sleeping in her bed when I entered her room and I crossed it to sit with her. I kissed her cheek. Max had been left to babysit Trissy and he wouldn't even know if she was ok. He didn't care much for babysitting his little sister. Even when it was to take his mother to the hospital. I hated him. More now than ever. I tucked Trissy in and left to go to my own room, climbed onto my bed and just sat looking out the window at the 4 little white crosses in the graveyard. "Who are you?" I asked myself. I turned to climb into my bed and there, sitting on the edge of it was a little girl. She was pretty. I could almost see right through her. She whispered "Tell them!" I didn't know where she had come from or how she got there and I didn't understand what she was saying. "Tell who?" She faded away in front of my eyes. Then she was gone. This was the first time I actually saw her and I knew! I just knew what it was I had to do.

CHAPTER 9

TRISSY

Trissy was a meek and mild 2 year old who didn't say much. Actually she said nothing at all. My little sister was mute. She was born with a voice, but our family dog, Buster, turned one day, out of the blue whilst we were playing in the back yard and attacked her. I tried to fend him off but he kept going, he was like a dog with a bone. He didn't even have a reason. He almost killed her. He ripped at her throat and when they surgically closed it up we were told she'd never speak again. I'd never hear her say anything, ever again. That was something that rocked my world. It was until this exact evening that I came to the acceptance I would never be able to converse with my sister. Trissy was always running around and playing with her toys, she was a loner though. She'd prefer to sit in her room and listen to her kid's shows on her iPad, with her ears filled with ear phones. She wasn't your typical 2 year old though, either. She would dress herself, feed herself and even put her own shoes on but someone would have to do up the laces, she wasn't that smart. "It's as if she is a grown up in a little body", I used to think to myself. I loved her. She never knew how much, really, until the night I saved her from the dog. Still, something kept bothering me. It didn't take me long to figure out what that was.

I was walking past Trissy's room this particular night and I could have sworn I heard voices. "How's that possible?" I thought. "That's impossible!" I thought again. I pushed open the door and out of the corner of my eye, I could have sworn I saw something or someone move. "I must have been hearing things!" I resolved. "There's no way on this god given earth, I was hearing Trissy, she can't talk". I did actually say 'voices', plural. Trissy was sitting on the floor, having a tea party. She looked so little in the moon light that was streaming through her window. I had to take a second glance as I honestly thought I saw another face, not Trissy's. I couldn't be sure and then it was gone. "It must be the light playing tricks on me." I said, to myself and left the room.

CHAPTER 10

THE CELLAR

I decided to explore the house. I opened each door as I came across it. Nothing seemed ominous in any of them. They were your regular rooms. Bedrooms, dining room, study and library. Nothing out of place, "Mother keeps everything nice." I uttered to myself. "Everything has a place." I remembered what my father use to say. "Hmmmm!" "Maybe that's why." I was meandering along the hallways when I came across a door. "I don't think I've ever seen this one before." I said to myself. I stepped closer to it and put my hand on the handle. A shiver ran down my spine. I couldn't stop from feeling that I'd done this before. Almost like a feeling of dejevu even. I went to turn the handle when I heard a 'thud' from behind it. Then the running of feet. This made me step away from the door but something was telling me to 'go in', before I got the chance to turn around and run, I felt propelled toward it and I couldn't control my actions. I was being 'made' to enter the room. In my own mind, I knew which room it was. It was the cellar. The same one that boy was telling those kids about in the school yard that day. The one where those children's bodies were found. Dead!. I was afraid. Terrified, for a better word. I turned the handle and pushed open the door.

I began to walk down the stairs and I fumbled for a light switch on the wall. I couldn't find one. There seemed to be enough light coming into the cellar. Just enough to see where I was going but not enough to see what was below. It was as if I was the light. Hard to explain but it seemed the light shed as I walked. "Hmmmm" I thought.. "strange!" When I reached the bottom of the stairs, my eyes filled with the sights that lay before me. In one corner was an old, tattered, mattress. I didn't know how long it had been down here but it looked like it had been for years. In another corner there was a chain attached to a wall. I decided it may have been a dog that lived here at some time. The mattress was it's bed and the chain would have been attached to it's collar. How wrong I was!.

The cellar was really cold and I shivered as I took a look around. I could feel eyes on me. I knew I was being watched. I just knew.

I found lots of little things in this room and before I got a chance to explore further, my search was disrupted by a ghostly vision that hankered in the corner. I could see the little girl was the same one that appeared to me on my bed. I slowly edged towards the figure and she began to scream. I said "shhhhhh," "I'm not going to hurt you!". "I promise." and reached out to take her hand. My hand fell straight through hers. "Ummm", I realised, although I already knew, that she was an apparition. She looked at me with tear filled eyes and said, "You must tell them!" "Tell them what?" I didn't exactly know what it was I was supposed to know. She tried to stand up. She couldn't. It was then I saw it. There was a chain attached to her ankle. I'd say if I was to describe it, a ghostly chain. "I carry this around with me and have done for many years." This little girl told me her name was Lucy. I sat in the corner with Lucy and listened as she told me her story.

CHAPTER 11

LUCY

"I was only eight when we came to live in this house." My parents bought it when they finished saving, for many years, to buy one, It was a lovely house." "I used to run and play in the yard and I had my own room." "It was the one that over looked the graveyard" "The one you have now". I listened to Lucy as she told me how she went missing about a year after moving into her house. She was playing in the front yard one morning, before school, a man approached her at the front gate and told her he was looking for his puppy. He asked her if she would help him look. Lucy loved puppies! So she walked out of the gate, hand in hand, and was never seen again. That was not until she was found, dead, in this cellar. She went on to tell me that there were others just like her. They all disappeared the same way. All were found, dead, in this cellar. As soon as a child would go missing, they searched this cellar, and sure enough there they were. They were found chained to the wall like dogs. I listened to the whole story and before

I knew it there were other ghostly figures gathering around us. I lost count on how many but I could say at least eight.

Lucy introduced me to them all. They were of different ages and different backgrounds. Boys and girls. All of a sudden I recognised one of the faces. Then two, three and four. They were Trixie, Missy, Adam and Ben. There was also another face in the midst that I didn't recognise. I said, "You must be Troy!" He nodded. Missy glared at me and I felt like her eyes would strike me down where I stood. She was a rather nasty looking girl. I couldn't believe my eyes, so many kids were now gathering around me. But for some strange reason, I knew! I just knew!

After I had spoken with the dead kids for what seemed like a very long time. I had the full story and I promised I would do something about it. After all I was the only one alive to do so. This would be my first, worse, mistake amd it may have been my last.

CHAPTER 12

THE GRAVEYARD

I left the cellar and all the spirits of the kids remained trapped there. I found out that the 4 little white crosses were actually those of Trixie, Missy, Adam and Ben. They had been found, dead, in the cellar of the house we lived in. They told me that their spirits lived in the fireplace, that was until my father lit the fire that night. They told me that they tried to stop him. "We tried to lock him out!" "Let him freeze to death". "We even tripped him over and hoped he would split his head open and bleed to death" Ben said with no remorse. "In the end we decided." We planted the thought in his mind and he left." "He destroyed what we loved, our home, as soon as he lit the fire." "So we destroyed his home by making him leave". "Now we are all in limbo" I thought to myself, "but aren't you all in limbo now?" I didn't ask.

They told me that they also made my mother pour the kettle over her own hand. When I asked them why? They told me, "she doesn't like you much!" I agreed. I did, however tell them, "I love her, regardless." They seemed amused by this and just laughed.

They asked me what had happened to Trissy... I told them the whole sad story about the dog attack and they laughed again... "we talk to her every night." They all chimed in together and said. "How?" I asked. But I knew, I just knew.

"And Max?" They knew what I was referring to. "Yep!" "Him too" they laughed again.

I felt like I had an entourage and they were all looking out for me. I thought they 'had my back'. How wrong I was.

The next morning I was sitting on the steps of our front porch, before school and just like they said it would happen, an old man walked over to me, he looked like he'd spent his nights on the streets, homeless would describe the shabbiness he seemed to portray. His clothes were ripped and he had a jacket on that was covered in dirt. "He looked up and I saw his face, it was ugly. It was covered in scars, like that of a man who had narrowly escaped a fire. He had big, wide eyes that seemed to lack life. His hair was black and matted, he looked like he hadn't showered in years, and he smelt bad. He told me he had lost his puppy and asked me to help him look for it. I told him I wasn't allowed to speak to strangers and that he looked like someone not to be trusted. Then before I knew it I was being propelled forward. I tried to resist but it was useless. I was made to get up and start walking towards this stranger and we walked out the gate and down the road. I was scared. I tried to stop but it was as if I wasn't in control of my own body, let alone my feet. I just kept walking next to him. He grabbed my hand. I tried to pull it away. I couldn't.

He gripped it so hard, it hurt. We walked a little way and then he turned around. He struck me with his big, dirty fist and I lost consciousness. No one saw this happen and when I awoke I was in the cellar. It was dark. I couldn't see anything around me. I had a chain attached to my ankle and the other end to the wall.

I was in pain. I could feel the blood as it trickled down my forehead and into my eyes.

I wondered "what now?".

The ghost kids all began to appear out of no where. I was just like them. But I wasn't. I was alive. Trixie came over to me and placed her hand on my shoulder. "You know what you have to do now!" She said. "Yes!" "I know!" I tried to stay awake but lost consciousness again.

When I awoke for the second time he was looming over me. "Who are you?" I asked him. He looked at me with the big black eyes and spat in my face as he spoke.

I used to be the gardener at the cemetery, that is until those pesky kids made me lose my job. I used to come to work, tend to the flowers that loved ones would put on the graves. I mowed the lawn and kept the place looking spic and span. Then one morning I left for work and when I got there I found the graves had been turned over. The tomb stones had been desigrated and all the flowers on familie's graves were ripped apart. "Those damn kids had a ball that night". He told me. I could see the ghostly figures of the kids as they gathered in the room. He was unaware of their presences and I knew. I just knew!

The man went on to tell me his name was John. He had a family of 3 littlies and a lovely wife named Susan. They were a happy little family until the fire. Shortly after, the fire had claimed the lives of all of them, John lost everything. Not only his family but his home and his darling pet puppy, he had just bought the girls for their last birthday. He also lost his mind. I could sort of gather the whole story now and it was so different from the one I had been told from the ghost kids. It wasn't the same at all!.

John told me "I accepted that I'd lost them but when I was blamed for the fire, that's when I swore I would get my revenge." "I killed those pesky kids, one by one, over 4 weeks." Then as I knew this house was close to the cemetery, somewhere I could gain access to quickly, I lured them away with the pretence of looking for my puppy." "Kids love puppies." "Don't you!" He directed this last statement at me. "Yes!" "We do" I replied.

The kid ghosts all began to gather around as the story from John was being told. I could see what they were about to do. I didn't know wether I actually felt sorry for them or for John. I didn't get a chance to decide.

John's eyes bulged, almost out of his head, he was having the life sucked out of him. These kids and I had derived a plan to end the killings. Little did I know I would be the last victim to tell the story. In the rooms upstairs there were lying 3 bodies. One in her bed, she seemed to be sleeping, however there was no breath left in her body. The second sitting in a chair with a face the shade of midnight blue, in front of his computer with earphones in and the third, a woman who had run a bath, stepped in and 'accidently' fell, hitting her head on the side of the bath and leaving a trail of blood as it dripped down the side and onto the white tiles.

I didn't know they were there. All I knew is I'd been used to lure this man, who I'd decided, wasn't all that mean, to our cellar. The place where I would take my last breath amongst all the mischievous little imps that lived in our house.

On the ground before me was his body, all the air had been sucked out of his lungs, he lie with half a smile on his face. And here I was chained to the wall, amongst all the ghost kids who at one stage were in the same situation. The difference was I was still alive.

Or was I? I knew! I just knew!

After what seemed like many years had gone by and the stigma of the house had been washed away with time. The house on the edge of the graveyard was sold.

A man and a woman with two little girls, aged 5 & 8, had bought it. They had a big black car and a dog named Charlie.

The little girl, named Susie, was so excited to be having her own room. She jumped up on her bed and looked out the window. There at the edge of the graveyard she could see 5 little white crosses. She thought to herself. "They don't look right!" "It looks like no one loved them." and in the air around her, she thought she could hear the faint sound of children giggling.

How right she was!

The end.

COMPLETED May 20/5/2019

THE STORYTELLER

CHAPTER 1

ELLE STARK

Elle Stark was just a little girl when she began to tell stories. She would often sit with other kids at lunch time at school and entertain them with tales of wonder. Elle didn't know where all her concepts came from but she did know that the tales she told were amusing and would often make the other kids laugh or cry or cringe when the stories were horrid. Elle loved to hear others giggle when they would sit in a circle and listen.

Elle was considered by others, to be a liar. She preferred to call herself a story teller. She would often read books from the library written by great fairy tale authors. She vowed to one day become a great author herself. She never thought the life she was about to live in would afford her all the stories she needed to one day be that great writer she so badly desired to be. When Elle was a little girl she would tell lies. Not huge lies. Little white ones that harmed no one.

That was until her life changed and all the stories she began to tell were told from experience.

Elle's life was about to take a twisted turn and her stories would no longer be told from fiction. They would now be told from fact.

When Elle left home at the young age of 15 due to the irreconcilable differences she had with her parents, she met Eddy. Elle thought her life was that out of a fairytale. He would dote on her and bring her chocolates and flowers every weekend. He would run her a bath on the Friday night after she'd finish at work. Elle wrote for the New Hampstead Times. She was a journalist. A free lance writer.

Elle took her job very seriously. She would report the stories just as they happened. Then when she got home she'd write her own short stories. She would often mix fact with fiction of the true events that occurred in her own life and embellish her stories to make them sensationalized to compose them.

She never considered that these were untruths, after all they were just stories. With an element of truth wrapped into them.

One Friday evening she was soaking in the bath that Eddy had drawn for her in their two bedroom unit earlier. The typical event that took place on a Friday night. When she'd finished her bath she wrapped a towel around her naked body and headed into the dining room. There they were the flowers and chocolates that she had grown accustomed to receiving. But something felt different, something was wrong, where was Eddy.

Usually Elle would step out of the bath and into a towel held open by her wonderful boyfriend. He would wrap the towel around her and his huge arms and give her a tight squeeze. Then they would both head into the dining room where he would present her with a beautiful bunch of roses, usually a dozen red ones and a yummy box of chocolates. Her favorite of course!

All the above mentioned were sitting on the dining room table. But Eddy was nowhere to be seen. "Maybe he's ducked into town to get something for dinner". Elle thought to herself.

It wasn't like Eddy to not be there when she got home. But she considered the possibility he would return shortly. "Maybe he's just ducked out for some ice." She thought to herself.

After the third hour had passed and still no sign of Eddy, Elle checked her phone again. "That's weird!" She whispered to herself. "He's never gone this long!" "Maybe something's happened!"

Elle rang a couple of Eddy's mates. "Have you heard from Eddy?" She asked Tod. "No! sorry!" Tod replied. "Have you called Max?" "No!" "Not yet!" Elle was beginning to worry.

Soon after Eddy had been gone for nearly 5 hours. No word from him and no idea of where he could be, Elle rang the authorities.

"My boyfriend is missing!" She told the sergeant on the phone. "How long has he been gone?" "About 5 hours or so" Elle told the man on the phone who was now known as Sergeant Luke Moss. "It's not like him to be gone this long!" Elle couldn't hold back the tears that had begun to crawl down her cheeks.

"I'm really not too sure where he could be or even if he is ok!" Elle continued.

"Well!" Sergeant Moss told Elle. "We cannot put out a missing persons report until he's not been seen or heard of for 24 hrs." "I'm sure he'll come waltzing through the door before you know it, with some cock and bull story of where he's been!" "They usually do." Sergeant Moss was laughing, a horrible laugh that Elle would get to know too well.

"Ok!" She replied. "I'll wait until morning and then I'll call you again if he's still not home." "24 hours." Moss reminded her. "Not an hour earlier."

Elle didn't like the man on the other end of the phone. "You don't know Eddy like I do!" She put down the phone and headed to bed.

CHAPTER 2

NEXT MORNING

When Elle woke at 2am she rolled over hoping to see her wonderful boyfriend lying next to her. The bed was empty. It hadn't been slept in. "Where are you?" She asked the ceiling as she looked up. She patted the pillow next to her. Picked it up and smelt it. The aroma of Eddy's pheromones wafted into her nostrils. She really loved his smell and she placed the pillow beneath her head. She drifted back off to sleep. At 4am her phone dinged. She was sleeping and thought she may be dreaming. She ignored it. When Elle finally woke she glanced at her phone and saw the missed message that she had ignored earlier. It was from Eddy. "Omg!" She squealed. "I missed his call." "At least he tried, he's alive!" She jumped out of bed and headed to the bathroom. It was 7am. After relieving herself she undressed and stepped into the shower alcove. "I wonder where he is!." Her shower was delightful. Elle allowed the warm water to trickle down her back. She decided to do a zen meditation session. She closed her eyes. Imagined the water as it careened down her face, over her breasts and down her abdomen. Elle took herself away from the mundane place she was in. She allowed the water to wash down her back and imagined herself standing on a shore. She could feel the warmth of the sun on her face and could feel the wind in her hair. Elle could smell the salt in the air and felt the hot sand beneath her feet. She delighted in being in this beautiful place of serenity. Elle decided it was time for a holiday. "When Eddy gets home we'll go away somewhere where we can be alone." she thought to herself. Elle didn't hear her phone ringing. She stepped out of the shower alcove and reached for a towel which she had hung on the heated towel rail before stepping into the shower. It wasn't there! Elle was confused. "I could have sworn I put a clean towel there." "Am I going crazy?" Elle put on her dirty pj's she had taken off and walked into her room. There sitting in a chair next to the window was Eddy. She saw the colour had drained from his face. Actually "He looks DEAD!" She screamed. Blood was trickling from the corners of his lips. Elle raced over to him and wrapped her arms around his neck. It had been slashed. The blood ran freely down his chest. Soaking his white shirt in crimson red. Elle fell to his feet.

Elle began screaming. The next door neighbour must have heard her and began banging on the front door. It wasn't closed. The door fell open. Mrs Harmer was an older woman of around 70. She couldn't believe her eyes when she entered the room Elle was screaming from. Elle was sitting at the foot of a man who seemed to be dead. The blood had begun to pool under the chair as it dripped on the floor from his slashed neck. Mrs Harmer didn't know what to think.

Had this woman, she barely knew Elle, killed this man? Had she found him sitting, dead, in this chair? Mrs Harmer crossed the room and wrapped her arms around Elle. "What's happened?" She asked Elle. "I don't know!" Elle was sobbing wildly. She couldn't explain because she honestly didn't know.

Elle began to tell Mrs Harmer, when she managed to calm her sobbing, that Eddy had been missing. He didn't come home but he did ring her and she missed his call. She continued. "I stepped in and had a long, hot shower and I did a zen meditation." Mrs Harmer looked at her incredulously. "So you're one of those spiritual types are you?"

Elle looked back at her. "Yes!" I practice meditation every day and I centre myself every night." "I also do yoga every weekend and tai chi when I've got free time." "So yes!" "You could call me a spiritual type." "Is that ok?" She didn't mean to sound so rude. "I'm sorry!" Mrs Harmer told Elle. "I meant no ill intent." "I just meant are you spiritual?" "Sorry." "I just felt a little trapped with that question." "Not many people in this neighbourhood know what I do." "Oh!" "But you're wrong young lady, very wrong."

"We all know you write!" Elle was taken aback with this. She didn't even realise she was known to be a writer. She lived a quiet existence and didn't really think anyone cared. Not enough to know who she was anyway, least the fact they knew she was a writer.

Elle picked up her phone and rang "911" The voice on the other end replied. "I'd like to report a murder!" Elle broke down in tears and handed the phone to Mrs Harmer.

CHAPTER 3

THE BODY

When the police arrived the first voice Elle heard was Sergeant Moss, he wasn't laughing. A policewoman called Constable Trudy Ellis took Elle aside. Mrs Harmer was directed into another room and a group of men and women crowded into the bedroom. By this time, Eddy's body had been zipped up in a body bag and was being wheeled out the door by the coroner.

"Time of death was somewhere in between 6 and 7 this morning." Maybe a little after but not any later than 8." "How could that be?" I have been here the whole time." "In the shower." Elle, glanced at her watch it was just after 10. "He was killed in this room!" A shiver ran down her spine, then she remembered the missing towel. "The killer was in my bathroom." She swallowed hard and almost vomited with the thought.

The police ran an in depth forensics of the entire room. They couldn't find the murder weapon. After a couple more hours of searching inside and outside the unit. "There's nothing!" Elle heard Sergeant Moss telling the other forensic officers. "There's no weapon." "No evidence that there was even another person in the room." "Is it possible that Elle killed him." Elle heard her name and realised she was a suspect in the murder of Eddy. She swooned and fainted.

When Elle came around she was lying on her bed. She was still wearing the pj's she was in when she fainted. "Was it a dream?" She asked herself. She climbed out of bed. No one was in the room. If it was a dream then why did it look like a murder scene. There was yellow and black ribbon tied across her front door when she opened it to step outside. "No!" "It was real!" Elle closed the door and headed back into her dining room. She was thirsty. She realised that she hadn't eaten since she woke up and began to make a sandwich. It was then that she noticed the knife missing from her knife block. "Hmmm!" She mused. "I wonder where that could be?"

She then had the darkest thought enter her mind. "Was it used to kill Eddy?" "She picked up her phone to call Sergeant Moss and dropped the phone. It landed with a thud on the ground. There it was. The handle of the knife that was missing, sticking out of the ground in front of the big tree in her back yard. "How did they miss that?" She whispered to herself. "No way!" "It sticks out like dog's balls." "They couldn't have missed it!" Elle ran outside to retrieve the knife. When she stooped to pull it out of the ground. Elle saw it. There was blood all over the knife handle and all over the blade. It was red and sticky and she could feel it all over her hand when she held the knife handle. She dropped it on the ground. "This is the missing knife that killed Eddy!" She couldn't breathe. She found it very hard to inhale and felt herself beginning to swoon again. She managed to hold on until she ran back inside. Banging her head on the door as she stood inside the front hall. She fell.

CHAPTER 4

WHO KILLED EDDY?

When Elle came around again, she was lying in her bed. "How did I get here?" "I remember falling at the front door. "I'm so confused!" Elle was feeling very light headed. She lost consciousness again. This time when Elle woke she was still lying in her bed but this time she was naked. She couldn't remember undressing. "What's happening to me?" "Am I going crazy?" These were questions she didn't know how to answer. When Elle began to climb out of her bed she noticed her phone on the desk near the window. She couldn't remember putting it there. She crossed her room and picked up her phone. There were twelve missed calls. Every one from Eddy. "What?" She dropped the phone and screamed. "How?" "This isn't possible!" "He's dead!" "I saw him!" " I saw him in the chair!" "I saw him zipped up in the body bag!" Elle realised she was rambling to herself. "How's this possible?"

"It isn't!" A familiar voice was heard behind her. It was the voice of Sergeant Moss. "Why is this happening?" Elle asked the man who was sitting in the chair that she had earlier found Eddy sitting in with his throat slashed. "Eddy is dead!" "Isn't he?" "Yes." "He's dead!" Sergeant Moss tipped his head to the side and Elle could see that he was holding the knife that she had earlier dropped outside. "I found this outside!" Sergeant Moss said matter of factly. "How did it get there?" "I don't know!" Elle was afraid. Here was Sergeant Moss sitting in the chair that her boyfriend had been found dead in and he was acting "Weird." Elle whispered the words so that she could be only one to hear them. "Why are you in my room?" She asked Sergeant Moss. "How did you get inside?" "The door was unlocked!" Elle didn't know if he was telling the truth or lying. She challenged him. "I locked the door!" "I'm sure I did!" "Are you calling me a liar?" Sergeant Moss seemed a little offended. "No!" "I'm just saying!" Sergeant Moss got up from his chair and headed towards Elle. All of a sudden he lunged at her and knocked her to the ground. He pinned her down and sat on top of her. His hands reached for her neck. "You're the liar!" Elle was struggling to breathe. "You reported on a story that got my brother locked away for life." "He's going up for the death penalty next week, and there's nothing anyone can do!" "You and your lies!"

Elle couldn't get enough breath to answer his accusations. She couldn't even remember which story he was referring to. She gasped. From behind Sergeant Moss she could just make out a large object being swung through the air. Then just as she lost consciousness from the huge hands being wrapped around her throat she saw her. Mrs Harmer.

CHAPTER 5

WHO KILLED SERGEANT MOSS?

When Elle gained consciousness she was lying in her bed. She was covered in blood. On the ground at the foot of the bed was Sergeant Moss. Mrs Harmer was sitting in the chair that Eddy had been killed in. The knife that Sergeant Moss was holding before he lunged at her was lying on the ground. The large object, being a statue, was lying next to Sergeant Moss's dead body. Mrs Harmer crossed the room and sat on the bed next to Elle. She took her in her arms and hugged her.

Sirens in the background were screaming and she could hear voices approaching her room. The same police forensics team were stepping through the door. This time there were a couple of different ones. Elle hadn't seen these men before. They were telling each other that there was another dead body in the same room they were in this morning. "This girl's been busy!" She heard them saying to each other. Mrs Harmer was still sitting on the bed when the police walked in.

Elle sat and watched the activity in the room. She could see the dead body on the ground and she observed Sergeant Moss's body. The statue that Mrs Harmer had struck him with was no longer lying next to Sergeant Moss's body. "Where was the statue?" She asked herself. Mrs Harmer looked at her incredulously. "What statue?" She asked. Elle realised she had actually said this out loud. "The one you hit Sergeant Moss with." "What?" "The one I hit him with?" "You hit him!" I stopped you from smashing his skull in!" Elle was so confused. "I don't know what's happening!" Elle began to cry again. Mrs Harmer got up and walked across the room and sat in the chair next to the window again. "You're a liar!" She whispered to Elle. "You tell lies and people believe you." "They think you are the bees knees." "You are just a compulsive liar and everyone believes your lies." "I'm a storyteller!" Elle said in her own defence. "I tell stories!" "I don't lie!" "Sometimes I take a piece of information or a piece and I embellish it." "But I don't lie!" Mrs Harmer slapped Elle across the face. "You're going to jail!" "You can write your stories from a jail cell!" "Why?" "What did I do to you?" Mrs Harmer stood up and walked out the door.

CHAPTER 6

ARRESTED

Once the police forensics team had left Elle was still lying in her bed. There was a silence that fell across her room. Not a sound could be heard anywhere. No birds sung in the trees. There was no wind outside, the trees were still. Elle sat in her bed and looked out the window. Outside, in the front yard, the police cars were pulling away. Elle glimpsed the face of Mrs Harmer in the back seat of one of the cars. "Mrs Harmer?" Elle yelled out. "What?" "Why?"

A policewoman stepped into Elle's room. "We found the knife that was used to kill Eddy!" "We then found the statue that was used to kill Sergeant Moss." "Mrs Harmer held a grudge against you!" "Do you remember a story you wrote about 5 years ago?" "It was about the fire that was started in the cellar of the house down the road?" Elle tried to remember. "Please, refresh my memory she told the policewoman." "You wrote a story about a house down the road, the fire started in the cellar and a man was killed in the fire." "That was Mrs Harmer's husband, Ian." Elle could slightly recall the story the policewoman was referring to. "He had a still in the cellar, he was making Whiskey."

The fire started as an accident from the still exploding and you wrote the story saying it was an insurance claim." "It wasn't" "It was a simple accident." Mrs Harmer couldn't claim her home on insurance because of the story you told." "When she completely lost her sanity, she honed in on you, The Storyteller." "If it wasn't for you she would have proved it an accident and she could have claimed her insurance." Elle couldn't believe what she was hearing. It was her fault. Incidentally but still her fault.

"When Mrs Harmer found out that Sergeant Moss also had it in for you because of your story that put away his brother, she collaborated with him to kill your Eddy." Sergeant Moss must have had a change of heart and when he approached Mrs Harmer telling her to let it go." "Mrs Harmer lost her mind and killed Sergeant Moss."

"Mrs Harmer hoped it would be pinned on you but she didn't count for Sergeant Moss's confession." Elle listened to what she was saying. "Sergeant Moss wrote a letter of confession." "When Sergeant Moss's body was found in your room, dead, it was a straight forward case of intent as he already divulged that you were innocent."

"The only thing you were guilty of, wasn't murder, it was lying!" "Or what you call it, being a story teller." After this the policewoman told Elle that she had been proven innocent. Mrs Harmer had given a full confession and now she had a true story to tell.

CHAPTER 7

THE STORY TELLER

Elle continued to be a free lance journalist. The only difference was she not only made sure that the stories she told were truth and nothing but the truth. Elle now had a very inside view of how a story could be misconstrued if it wasn't told exactly as it was.

She no longer embellished the truth. She told it as it was and made sure that she got the facts right.

Elle Stark was just a little girl when she began to tell stories. She would often sit with other kids at lunch time at school and entertain them with tales of wonder. Elle didn't know where all her concepts came from but she did know that the tales she told were amusing and would often make the other kids laugh or cry or cringe when the stories were horrid. Elle loved to hear others giggle when they would sit in a circle and listen.

Elle was considered by others, to be a liar. She preferred to call herself a story teller. She would often read books from the library written by great fairy tale authors. She vowed to one day become a great author herself. She never thought the life she was about to live in would afford her all the stories she needed to one day be that great writer she so badly desired to be. When Elle was a little girl she would tell lies. Not huge lies. Little white ones that harmed no one.

That was until her life changed and all the stories she began to tell were told from experience.

Now Elle sits at her desk day after day, night after night, writing the stories that she had experienced first hand. She no longer told little white lies. The title of her very first novel was called.

THE STORY TELLER.

The End

COMPLETED 18/8/2019

THE BOY IN THE CUPBOARD

CHAPTER 1

HE'S DEAD

"He was just a little boy!" He heard his mother's friend, Freda, telling the local sheriff. Little Tommy wasn't just a little boy. He was a very special little boy. But no one believed him when he told them, after many years of enduring what he went through, as he was "just a little boy". This little boy was now a big man and the memories he had locked away inside his mind were memories one may invite dementia into their life so as to forget. Little Tommy lived his life inside of a cupboard. He designed his existence within the 4 walls of his hallway closet. The only way he could escape was letting go of all the horrible memories he held in his head. This closet was the only thing that kept him safe. Even from his mad mother. But what would keep him safe now?

"Mummy", Tommy whispered. "Can I have some more?" and before he even got a chance to add the word please, he was swiped across the face with his mother's hand.

"Where is it that you are not taught to say please!" his mother roared. He grabbed his face where he had been slapped, which was burning and whispered "Please". "That's better", his mother said in a much less quieter voice also. "No!" There is no more", "You've got to leave some for your father". Tommy looked at his mother and began to form the words but he quickly decided it was better to say nothing. His mother was still angry and he didn't want another slap, the first one still stung, he decided to stay quiet and that way he wouldn't get into any more trouble. But, deep down inside he knew! His father had been killed in a train derailment on his way home from school one evening, 5 years ago. He was walking home from school and he saw the smoke in the distance from the train wreck, but he didn't know he was on it. He was told, by his neighbour, a friend of his mother, Freda, the next morning, that his father wasn't coming home anymore. He didn't cry. He felt relieved, his father use to beat him. He would lie in his room at night hearing his parents yelling and screaming at each other and as soon as he was almost asleep his mother would check to see if he was and his father would leave the house. Tommy never knew where he went but he did know his mother would be in the bathroom cleaning up her face, running a bath and soaking in the blood that was gushing from her wounds his father had caused. He would beat his mother and Tommy would quite often sneak out of his bedroom and down the hall. He would open the hallway closet door and step inside. Tommy felt safe when the walls surrounded him and he didn't have even enough room to move around. This is how Tommy had been living for the 10 years he was alive, so far. Until the day he was told his father wasn't coming home.

CHAPTER 2

MOTHER

Tommy's mother was known as mad to everyone. He even thought she was mad too. She would sit all day in her room and talk to herself. She would even answer herself at times and this just made her seem even madder. Tommy knew she would have been affected in some way after losing her husband in the train derailment. But he didn't know exactly to what extent she had been. He knew after many years of seeing his mother being brutally beaten that she would be feeling lots of emotions, just like he was, now that neither of them were being hurt. His mother started to get better, slowly, it took many years before she was completely healed. She stood in front of her dressing mirror this one particular day and reached out and smashed it. She then took a shard of glass from the pieces on the ground and put it to her throat. Little Tommy was standing in the doorway, he rushed into her room and gently took the glass from his mother, sat her on her bed and told her. "It's ok mum" "it's all over now". It was then that Tommy realised she had been damaged, more than anyone knew, but what caused her to do this 5 years later? Tommy would find out in the most terrifying way, what caused his mother to do all the things she did.

CHAPTER 3

THE ACCIDENT

Tommy didn't feel the need to climb inside the closet anymore. He wasn't hiding from his father and his mother had begun to be much nicer to him. He would pass by the door in the hallway and keep on walking. Never looking back and never feeling the urge to hide. Until the morning he was involved in a terrible accident.

He was riding his scooter, he'd gotten for his 15th birthday, on the front driveway and every now and then he'd do a complete circle which took him partially onto the road. A couple of times he would just be skimmed by a car coming around the corner. He was playing chicken. He got a thrill out of escaping each time and laughed when he saw the driver's face as it neared him and laughed even harder when he could see the terror in their eyes, the closer they got to him, the better the thrill.

Tommy must have misjudged the next car as it neared him and he could see the driver behind the wheel. He then realised this one had already been around the corner once. This time he didn't miss. He drove up onto the curb. Cleaning Tommy up. He went up and over the car bonnet. Then sped away. Tommy lie on the pavement in a pool of blood as it gushed from the wound on his head. He wasn't sure wether he was most scared of the car that hit him, or the face he saw behind the steering wheel, just before he lost consciousness he realised. "It was my father."

When Tommy came around he was surrounded by dazzling white lights and men and women in white coats. He wondered "Am I in heaven?" One of the women who was working on him, putting a brace on his neck and tightening the screws that were protruding from his head, looked at him and said "Don't try to move" "You've been hit by a car and you've broken your neck in 3 places." "Am I dead?" asked Tommy, "Where's my mother?" "She's on her way" he heard another man say. Then he lost consciousness again.

When he came around he was lying in a bed. He saw his mother sitting in a chair next to him. She was sleeping. He didn't want to disturb her and so he drifted back off to sleep. But not before he noticed the dark shadow lurking in the doorway of his hospital room. All he could see was the eyes. They were familiar to him. He couldn't tell who it was but he closed his eyes and tried to turn his head. He couldn't, it was held in place by a metal plate. He remembered the woman telling him "you've broken your neck in 3 places." He could feel the hot breath as it landed on his face. He could smell the distinct odour of alcohol and he knew it was his father. "He wants me dead." He allowed himself to zone out and fell asleep.

CHAPTER 4

THE CHAIR

The next day he heard the doctors telling the nurses "he'll never walk again!" That was it. His fate had been decided. He heard them all shuffling to and fro, in and out of his room. He fell in and out of consciousness and each time he noticed the dark shadow slinking in the corner. He allowed himself to go with it. He didn't try to stop as he drifted here and there and when he came face to face with the dark shadow he wasn't afraid anymore. They had already decided his fate. Didn't he get a choice? Didn't he have a say?

By the time he was totally aware of everything around him again, he had been gone for, the nurse told him, "20 years!" Tommy couldn't believe what he was hearing. "Twenty years?" He thought he'd heard them wrong. "Surely not!" He stared at them incredulously and the doctor said again "Twenty years" "you've been in a coma for that whole period of time" Tommy was shocked at what he was being told.

He wanted to be told he was dreaming. He wasn't. He learnt that whilst he was in the coma his mother sat next to him, day in, day out. "She never left your side!""She sat in that chair, over there" She pointed to the arm chair they'd bought into his room to offer comfort to his mother whilst she waited. The nurse told him. "She would talk to you, play you music and even sing to you." Where is she now?" Tommy enquired. "She's in heaven." "What do you mean?" Tommy asked the nurse. She told him that his mother became very ill and then she was diagnosed with breast cancer. She survived all the treatments and her journey looked like it was over. 7 years later she was told it had returned. She was given 12 months to live and every day she wished for him to wake up. "Why didn't I get put out of my misery?" He asked the nurse. "You weren't on a life support machine." "You were breathing for yourself" "Your mother made us promise you would not be let go unless you did go on a life support machine." "You never did" another Nurse had entered the room. "I could hear you, you know!" He told the nurses and "I wanted you all to know I was still inside but I couldn't." "I'd scream inside myself hoping you'd all hear me." "But you never did."

Tommy was given a complete check over and allowed to begin rehab as soon as his test results came back. He had to learn to walk again, talk again, properly and since he had aged for the 20 years he was comatose, he had to learn to shave. He laughed as he stared at the image in the mirror. A now 35 year old man. The face that stared back at him was that of an older man. Old! "Not bad!" He said to himself. "Not bad!"

He considered himself as old as he had gone into the coma at just being a little boy of 15 and emerged as a man of 35.

He was pushed out of the hospital in a wheelchair. He got to the end of the path and he was pushed in the chair to the car waiting for him. He recognised it as belonging to a friend of his mother. Her name was Freda.

CHAPTER 5

GOING HOME

Freda drove slowly, she weaved in and out of the traffic. She didn't say much on the ride home and Tommy didn't know what to say to her to begin a conversation. He didn't know this woman. He didn't remember much at all. His memory was the last thing that would return he was told by the doctors. He wondered if he would ever remember anything from his childhood. The child life he lived outside of the coma. She drove up the front drive and pushed a button on the remote she held in her hand. The garage door began to open and she drove the car inside. When Tommy saw the house he didn't recognise it. He didn't remember ever living there before. When he got out of the car he declined the use of the chair, quite adamantly he told Freda "I can do it!" He didn't mean to sound as harsh as he did but he couldn't take it back so he just began to head towards the door that led to the laundry. Or at least he thought it did. Freda directed him to another door way telling him things had been changed in his absence. "You're telling me!" He scowled.

Tommy entered the house he used to live in at 15. He walked past the doorway to the kitchen and as he passed the hallway closet door he stopped. He wanted to open it and look inside. He didn't know why or what the room even was. He just knew he had been here before. He turned the handle of the door and pulled it towards him.

When the door freed itself from the jamb it creaked. "It's getting old, just like me!" He joked. Freda didn't laugh, she didn't even smile. Tommy decided "You're a bit of a sour puss!" "Aren't you!" But he didn't say it out loud. Tommy stepped inside the tiny room. He asked Freda "I think I've been her before" "Do you know why I'm feeling like this?" "It's tiny." "Surely I didn't live in here" Freda didn't reply, she just walked away. In the corner of the tiny room Tommy saw something move. He could see a bit of light as it seeped in through the hallway closet door. Then all of a sudden he saw them. Two eyes looking straight at him. He thought he knew these eyes. But he couldn't remember who.

CHAPTER 6

THE SHADOW

Tommy asked Freda to leave once she'd helped him to unpack. He sat on his parent's bed and allowed himself to cry a little. He couldn't remember much about his childhood, except for the couple of times he heard a familiar dog bark or he'd enter into a room and get that feeling of dejevu. Like he'd been there before. Tommy would wander around the house remembering bits and pieces of his 35 years he'd been living. He would remember fragments of memories and even though he had photos hanging on the walls and sitting on mantle pieces, around him. They still didn't prompt his memory deep enough to know exactly what he had endured.

Then one night as he was settling into bed and was just about to turn out the light, he felt a presence in the room with him. He felt uneasy and knew something wasn't right.

He could smell a familiar smell that he just couldn't place. "Damn amnesia." He scolded himself for not being able to remember. A dark shadow formed next to his bed. He could see it like smoke. "I know I should remember." He told the shadow. "But I can't!" The shadow shifted and he saw those familiar eyes. The ones that appeared in the hallway closet. Again he knew he should've known who's they were.

Tommy was visited each night for the next few years. He had just turned 50 and he'd married a beautiful woman named Bella. He had a son who was 5 they called Peter and a daughter who was 8 they called Perl. The two kids would quite often run around the house and duck in and out of rooms as they played. Then one day they happened across the hallway pantry door. It opened, as they pulled it, with a loud creak. Tommy heard the sound of the door opening and recognised it as a familiar sound. He raced into the hallway and slammed the door shut. The kids were startled as to their father's actions.

"I don't want you ever to go in there!" He told his children. "Promise me you won't!" The kids just looked at their father and ran off down the hallway. Tommy closed the hallway closet door and just before it was completely shut he heard a sound from behind it. It was a soft whimpering, like that of a dog. "We don't have one!" He said to himself and let the door close fully.

CHAPTER 7

THE VOICE

Tommy was sitting on the front porch in his rocking chair, having a pipe when his children ran inside from playing in the garden. His wife Bella was in the kitchen preparing dinner when he heard a shrill scream come from inside the house. He ran inside to see what had happened, he thought Bella may have cut herself whilst cooking but he wasn't prepared for what he saw. Bella had been standing over the stove cooking when he stepped outside onto the porch and when Tommy entered the room he saw a sight for sore eyes. There hanging from the tree outside the window was the body of his son. Peter had hung himself and was hovering just above the ground. Bella was staring outside and before he knew it she picked up the knife she had been cutting the vegetables up with and plunged it into her chest. Not once, not twice but over and over again. Perl who came rushing into the kitchen after hearing the commotion, ran over to where her mother lie, lifeless on the kitchen floor. She took the knife out of her mother's chest and cut her own throat. Tommy stood in awe at the sight of the massacre. He was glued to the spot in which he stood. He could feel the presence at it formed around him. He closed his eyes. He ran. He ran to the hallway closet door and opened it. Fell inside and closed the door behind him. The handle broke. He slumped into the corner and stayed there unable to move. The black shadow loomed around him and two eyes stared into his. They were his father's eyes.

Freda opened the front door. After he hadn't answered the phone for 4 days she went to see if he was home. It wasn't like him to not get in touch and the family had organised a bbq the following weekend. Freda let herself in and walked into the kitchen. She screamed. There before her were the two dead bodies of Bella and Perl and outside the window was the half eaten body of Peter. It looked like it had been attacked by an animal of some sort. But where was Tommy? Freda rang the sheriff.

"He was just a little boy!" He heard his mother's friend, Freda, telling the local sheriff. He tried to scream out to them and tell them he was inside the hallway closet but he'd lost his ability to speak. He'd lost all his strength from fighting the black shadow that beat him about his face. His body was weakened and he had no will to fight any longer.

He could hear Freda trying to open the hallway closet door. "It must be locked!" She told the Sheriff. "I'm not sure where he is!" The sheriff asked "Do you think he did it?" "I don't know." said Freda.

Tommy lie in the corner of the hallway closet, behind a closed door whilst his family's bodies were being taken away in body bags. They never knew he was there and he was never seen again.

He could hear the sheriff asking Freda "Where is he?" Freda replied "He didn't come home" He's lying in a hospital bed in a facility" "it's been 40 years since he fell into the coma and they swore to his mother, before she died, that they would keep him alive as long as he was breathing by himself." "He still is!"

Tommy could hear what they were saying and he couldn't bring himself to utter a word. It was then he realised that the whole thing was just in his mind. He was still lying in the hospital bed. The one he was put in at the age of 15. He was still in a coma. No one died. He never married. Never had children. He never got out and lived the life he had imagined himself to live.

He glanced around and saw the eyes he now recognised to be his father's. He saw them as they veered the car into him and ran him down. He saw them as they stared at him as he was lying in the hospital, he saw the shadow slinking in the corner of his room.

Tommy lie in his bed and listened to the voices that surrounded him. He lay in a comatose state. No one ever unlocked the hallway closet door. No one ever let him out.

The end

COMPLETED May 29/5/2019

THE LAND OF CHOCOLATE & CANDY

CHAPTER 1

PLANNING TO ESCAPE

Mmmmmmm! Yummy! Mary wandered around her town. The delicious houses and trees and lakes and even the sky was made of chocolate. Who couldn't be happy in a place like this? Mary wasn't! She wanted so bad to leave this horrible place she lived in. Everyone around her delighted in waking up with their chocolate sun. Going to sleep with their chocolate moon and stars in the sky. When Mary decided she would escape this place she was born in, she found it almost impossible to do so. Every time she got near the huge chocolate gates and every time she even got close to catching a glimpse of what was beyond them, she fell. She would slide straight back to where she started from. Mary was doomed to live her life out in this sweet and sickly land of chocolate and candy.

Mary had other ideas. She would not stop planning how to get out. She would scribble it all down on a piece of chocolate paper, using a candy cane pen. All of a sudden she had a thought. What if I made a chocolate ladder and climbed over the wall made of rocky road? Then I could run as fast as I can into the, she stopped, what was beyond the chocolate gates. She didn't know! She was only remembering stories. Urban legends had been known to the towns people and often she would hear them saying "there's nothing out there!" "Anyway who wouldn't want to live here?, in this land of chocolate and candy. Mary didn't! Her mind often wandered off to places she thought would exist. Places that only existed in her mind. But she thought, "One day". "I'll get out of here!" "I'll run far away and I won't have to smell that sickly smell of chocolate".

Mary dreamed every night the same dream, over and over. The dream that had now become a nightmare. In this dream she would be running, she could hear the chocolate bears looming behind her and she could smell the liquorice sticks as they chased her. Mary was scared. She knew if she stopped running that the things chasing her would eat her. "But aren't I meant to eat them?" She thought. She kept running. This dream is the reason she hated living in this town. The sole reason she wanted to escape. She believed it would be the only way to make the dream stop.

She may have been right. But was she ever going to get the chance to find out?

CHAPTER 2

THE MASTER PLAN

Mary sat for what seemed like hours trying to define her master plan on how to escape. She scribbled down many theories and crumpled each one up as she realised they were fruitless. Then she came across something that caught her eye. It was a rope made from liquorice. It was lying in the corner of her room. She thought "If I can get to the top of the rocky road wall, then I can lower myself down using the liquorice rope", "Yes!" She exclaimed quite loudly. It was then she also noticed a shadow outside the window move. She was being spied on. She wondered how long he or she had been there. She truly hoped no one had heard her and to make sure she wouldn't be found out, she grimaced and ate her plans. "No one will ever know." "There's no evidence left behind, so no matter what that spy tells them. They can't prove it." Mary was quite pleased with herself and headed off to eat dinner.

That night she lie in her bed with a belly ache. "Ohhhhh!" "She said to herself" "I ate too much or something I ate hasn't agreed with me". "She ran to the toilet and began vomiting. What she saw in her vomit was a piece of the plans she had eaten. It showed the wall and the rope. She mustn't have chewed that piece enough, she decided. She flushed the toilet and a stream of lemonade took away the evidence. "Ah!" Mary uttered. "I feel much better now". But Mary didn't know how much trouble she would be in, especially when that piece of paper didn't dissolve and all toilet lemonade ended up at the recycling plant. Mary wandered back to her bed and fell asleep.

The next morning when Mary awoke she was disturbed by the voices outside her window. These voices were rather loud and seemed to be getting louder. She wondered what they were yelling about. She then heard a voice say "It was found this morning, by a worker at the recycling plant." "Someone's planning an escape!" Mary heard those words and shivered. "Oh my!" She thought. I should have chewed it more and instead of flushing it, I should have eaten it again." She knew this would send the town into a full scale panic mode. "Oh no!" She giggled to herself. "Someone's planning to escape." She couldn't help but shiver again, she remembered the shadow outside of her window. Someone knew! But who?

CHAPTER 3

THE SEARCH

Mary didn't want to get out of bed but she heard a sharp rap on her door. "Get up" the harsh voice demanded. "There's a huge search being conducted to find the would be escapee." She rubbed her eyes as she opened the door, yawned and said, "Wow!" "What can I do to help?" Pretending to be interested when all along she knew they were all searching, unbeknown to them, for her. "Get dressed and meet in the big hall" her visitor left her doorway without uttering another word. She put her hand to her head and clicked her heels together. "Yes Sir!" "Straight away Sir." She giggled a little to herself, began to close the door and was just about to turn around and begin getting dressed when a familiar figure appeared in her doorway. She couldn't see him or her very well as the chocolate sun was blazing in her eyes. But she heard the voice, it was a soft spoken child's voice. "I know it was you!" The little girl whispered and before Mary could say another word, she disappeared. Mary was a little bit frightened now. She thought someone knew and now she was certain. This was the same person who was outside her window. She hurriedly got herself dressed and headed for the big hall.

CHAPTER 4

THE BIG HALL

When Mary arrived at the big hall she couldn't believe what everyone was saying. She heard them all chattering about a would be escapee. She knew they were talking about her. "Who wouldn't want to live here?" She heard one woman ask. "It's perfect!" Another woman said. "Ungrateful bastards" "that's what they are." A man's voice was heard.

Mary stood in silence and listened as they all began to congregate in the big hall. This hall was made of ginger bread. It's windows were made from clear toffee. The doors and floors were, yep! You guessed it. Chocolate. Mary listened to all the different voices chiming together in the big hall and decided, even more determinedly than before. "I have to get out of here!"

Once everyone had gathered inside the big room they all began to yell and shout. "Ungrateful bastards!" The same woman repeated. " "Yep!" "They don't know how good they have it." Said another guy. Mary noticed a shadow lurking in the corner and just as she was about to head in its direction, it disappeared. She searched the whole room with her eyes and after about 5-10 mins she gave up. Many voiced they're opinions about the would be escapee and then the Mayor entered the room.

"Here Ye!" "Here Ye!" He shouted. Mary looked in his direction and could see he was short, stumpy, fat even. He wore a bright coloured pair of bloomers and a very dazzling coat over an equally bright coloured vest. "My attention has been bought to the would be escape attempt from our beautiful land of chocolate and candy" he continued. "Why would anyone want to leave this perfect place it is delicious, sweet, scrumptious" Mary could see the people gathered begin to salivate with what the Mayor was saying. Mary could taste a bitterness forming in her own mouth. She couldn't stand this town any longer. She stood up, straightened her back and pushed up her shoulders. She went to take a few steps forward but was headed off by the young girl who, she knew, knew who she was. The girl stood in front of her, reached up and gripped her shoulder.

Mary winced at the pain she was experiencing in the grip of the young girl. She was shocked by the strength this girl had. She tried to break free from her grasp but couldn't seem to even move an inch. The young girl whispered "If you leave now they'll know it's you!" She continued "If you stay here, with them, they will think you are one of them" "no one will know your intentions." "You won't be found out and you won't get caught"

Mary listened as the girl whispered these words and realised "you're right!" She whispered back.

Mary stood amongst the gathering and when the whole lot of bullshit speech had finally come to an end, she moved out of the hall with the rest of the townspeople. Mary hadn't changed her mind. She took heed of what the young girl had said and waited till the end. Mary scanned the group as they were heading out the door and searched for her 'advisor'. She couldn't see her and decided to head back to her room.

CHAPTER 5

BACK TO THE DRAWING BOARD

Mary arrived back in her room about 10-15 minutes after leaving the hall. She had full intentions of picking her plans of escape up where she left it. Then she noticed, as she neared her doorway, that it wasn't closed. Her door was ajar just a few centimetres and she knew something wasn't quite right. She had closed and locked it on the way out. She decided "someone's either been in, or is in, my room. She pushed the door open with caution. There behind it, in the half light of the chocolate moon, which streamed inside her room, she could see a figure sitting in her chair. She crossed the room slowly and as she neared the figure she could see it was "The little girl!" She let out a sigh of relief and continued across the room to where the little girl sat.

"Mary." She began. "I've been watching you for quite some time now and I'd say you've had enough!" "Am I right?" "Or am I right? "Hmmmmm?" Mary didn't know how to reply to this stranger sitting in her chair, in her room. "Yes!"

She whispered. "Pardon." Her visitor asked. "Pardon" she repeated, rather bossily. Mary repeated herself "yes!" She said a little louder this time, so as to be heard.

"Ok!" Her visitor took on the persona of a much older woman by this time. Mary began to see her in a different light. She was difficult to describe. But here goes. Mary saw the wrinkles which saturated her face and made her look a lot older than she had originally thought. She no longer portrayed a young child, she appeared to be 'growing up' before her very eyes. "How could this be?" Mary thought to herself.

Sure enough. Mary watched in bewilderment as her once young visitor now looked like a completely different person. "It's like magic." She uttered to herself.

"What's happening?" Mary asked her strange, she decided, new friend. "My name is Corinne" she began. I'm not who I appear to be. "No shit Sherlock!" Mary was stunned as she spoke those words. "It's ok! "I'm not who I appear to be because I'm you!" Mary looked at this once young girl, now turned woman, and could see that she was indeed turning into "Me!" She gasped. She was looking straight into a mirror image of herself. "I know you're shocked right about now" "Please!" "Let me explain!"

CHAPTER 6

MY MIRROR IMAGE

Corinne began by telling Mary "On the day you were born, here in this sweet town of chocolate and candy" "My mother, you're mother, also gave birth to me." "Our mother died during childbirth." "Did you know that?" Mary shook her head. She was remembering her father telling her that her mother had been very ill and when Mary was 2 years old, she had died of heart failure. She couldn't even fathom why her father would lie to her about the circumstances of her own mother's death. "Anyways", Corinne continued. "I was born as you" Mary couldn't make sense of what Corinne was saying. "I am your alter ego" "The other side of your brain which didn't develop" "That's me!"

Mary still struggled to understand what Corinne was telling her. She went on to say "When you were born, you had a brain disorder" "You tried to understand different things as you got older and as a result of the disorder, you developed a spilt personality" "That split personality, you decided would be given the name Candy" Mary stared at Corinne with open eyes. She was finding it very difficult to comprehend what this woman was saying to her. "Candy" She asked. "But you said your name is Corinne" "Yes!" You named me Candy and as you developed a hatred towards this beautiful place we live in, you decided to change it to Corinne." "You do know that's your, our, mother's name right?" Mary was still trying to get around the fact that she had actually made this woman and that she had imagined her to be real. Corinne stopped. Mary sat with tears in her eyes and asked "Corinne". "If you are me and I am me, then who are all the others in this town?" "How long have you lived inside of me?"

CHAPTER 7

THE ESCAPE

Mary stood at the door of her room. She stared out at the town before her. She could see gingerbread houses. Candy stick lamp posts. Liquorice roads. Candy trees. Lollipop flowers. The clouds in the sky were made of fairy floss. The huge wall around the whole town was made of rocky road and the sun and moon, in the night sky, "at the same time!" She noticed. These were made of chocolate.

Corinne had left her questioning her own sanity. "How could all this be true?" She decided it was just one big lie. Mary felt as if she had been stabbed in the chest. She could feel the pain as it was careening up her spine and into her head. Corinne appeared just a couple of short steps in front of her, smiling before fading away.

Mary closed her eyes and let herself fall. Her head hit the ground hard. Mary knocked herself out and when she woke she was lying in a bed. Not her bed, made of sweet candy, no! A stranger's bed. This one had cotton sheets and a bright coloured quilt cover, under which she lay. It had a soft pillow, not the one she was used to, this one felt like a nest of feathers beneath her head. She looked outside her bedroom window. What she saw blew her mind.

She could see brick houses. Metal lamp posts. Tarred roads. Green trees. Beautiful flowers. The clouds in the sky were white and fluffy but not made from fairy floss. The huge wall she could see around the town was made of bricks and the moon, in the night sky, wasn't made of chocolate, it was "different". She decided. "Where's the sun?."

Mary didn't know what to think. She kept glancing around the room, her room, it was painted pink with pretty purple, sheer, curtains. There on the opposite wall, was a dressing table. It was then she happened to glance in the mirror at her reflection. She no longer saw herself as little Mary. The image staring back at her was of a full grown woman. This woman didn't look like her but in a strange way, did.

A woman, unknown to her, walked into the room. Sat on her bed and said. "You're awake!" Mary thought to herself "yes!" "Where am I?" Mary asked the woman all sorts of questions. They just kept flowing out of her mouth. Before she knew it, she was telling this woman her whole story. The woman listened with wonder in her eyes. "So!" "The whole time you were 'away', you were living in your own land of chocolate and candy" "is this right?" "Yes!" Mary spoke with a waver in her voice. "You do realise you were born with a brain disorder, do you not?" "Yes!" "Corinne told me!" "Corinne?" The woman, who by this time, had explained that her name was Lesley, looked at Mary in a confused way. "Where did you get that name from?" Mary shuddered. She didn't know what Lesley was asking her. She didn't know how to explain it any further. "Isn't that what Corinne told me her name was?" She asked herself. She was sure her name was Corinne. Lesley took her hand. "Corinne was the name we gave to your sister" "she was your twin." "She died in childbirth when your mother Mary died"

Mary looked at Lesley and asked her the question she had on her lips. "Then who am I?" She didn't know whether or not she wanted to hear the answer to that question. Lesley took her in her arms and patted her back. Your name is Candy. Mary fell into the embrace of Lesley's arms. She cried rivers of tears that she felt had been bottled up for so long. When she had finally managed to compose herself and after what seemed, an eternity, she pulled away from Lesley and sat bolt upright. "So then!" She began. "It was all just a dream!"

Lesley gently touched her face and whispered. "No!" "If you believe that's where you've been" "Then that's where you've been."

Mary, who now knew herself as Candy. Looked on as the doctors and nurses bustled there way around her room. She came to learn she was in a facility for the mentally ill. She also learned that as a result of her brain disorder she was born with, that all the time she believed she was living in her 'fantasy land' as Mary, she was in fact a drug addict. She had been taking them all her life. She had begun at the young age of 12 and from that moment on she couldn't define reality from her fantasy land she lived in.

Candy was given treatments to help her kick her addiction and these treatments included brain wave shock treatment. This altered her brain waves and it affected her brain in ways that only she knew were possible. She learned that after her mother's death and the death of her twin sister Corinne. That she went off the rails and began exhibiting strange behaviours.

Candy received countless sessions of psychotherapy and after what seemed, to Candy, to have taken forever, which in actual fact took 12 months or more, as well as brutal bashing's from inmates and sexual attacks from the facility staff. A near death overdose that had been forced upon her and a broken nose from trying to protect herself from the bullying that she was receiving after dark from her cell mate. She felt like she was living in a prison, she was released from captivity. She was cured. No longer did she experience any drug induced psychosis episodes.

She had them convinced she was a 'normal thinking human being'. She walked down the road that led to the gates.

There at the end of the pathway she stood. She stared up at the sky. The clouds above her were white and fluffy made of fairy floss. She could see gingerbread houses in the distance. Candy stick lamp posts. Liquorice roads. Candy trees. Lollipop flowers. The huge wall around the town was made of rocky road and the sun and moon, in the night sky, "at the same time!" She smiled. These were made of chocolate.

Candy who had changed her name to Corinne. Had fooled everyone into believing she had been cured. Sure! She was no longer an addict. She no longer took drugs to induce her fantasy land to appear.

Corinne skipped down the roads made of liquorice and she picked the lollipop flowers along the way. She ran up and hugged a tree made of candy. She licked it. "Mmmmm" it tastes so good." She giggled. She swung herself around and around the candy stick lamp post and she laughed to herself. "Maybe!" "Just Maybe" "This land of candy and chocolate isn't so bad after all." She heard the cheering of the townspeople and she saw the mayor in his brightly coloured clothing coming towards her. She ran down the streets and when she reached her house, she kicked her heels up. Opened the gate made of chocolate, ran up to the door made of ginger bread and rushed inside.

"Maybe!" "Just Maybe!" This is the best place on earth to be.

"No shit Sherlock!" She heard the voice come from inside her. She laughed out loud and ran over to her bed. Threw herself on it and laughed until she fell asleep.

Corinne dreamed of all the wonderfull things she could do in her land made of chocolate and candy.

The end

COMPLETED May 29/5/2019